JESSICA BECK
THE DONUT MYSTERIES, BOOK 50

BAKER'S BURDEN

Donut Mystery 50 BAKER'S BURDEN
Copyright © 2020 by Jessica Beck
All rights reserved.
First edition: 2020

The First Time Ever Published!
The 50th Donuts Mystery
BAKER'S BURDEN

Jessica Beck is the *New York Times* Bestselling Author of the Donut Mysteries, the Cast Iron Cooking Mysteries, the Classic Diner Mysteries, the Ghost Cat Cozy Mysteries, and more.

WHEN A WICKED LANDLORD is murdered during a going-out-of-business sale in April Springs, everyone who runs a business in the strip mall he owns is a suspect, including one of Suzanne's good friends. Not only that, but there are even more folks from town who are under scrutiny as well. As Suzanne and Grace dig into the murder, they must do their best not to be the killer's next victims, too.

To you, my loyal readers, for sticking with me through fifty donut books,
Each one of you is golden to me!
And of course, always and forever,
To P and E

Chapter 1

IT STARTED OFF AS A day of sadness but also one of celebration, a witness to the end of one dream and the hope of a new beginning taking its place, but all of that took a back seat when murder paid another visit to the small and cozy town of April Springs, North Carolina.

"Jenny, I need to get into the storage room," I told the owner of For The Birds, the specialty shop that was going out of business. Jenny Preston had emulated my behavior when she'd opened her store, and there were more parallels between us besides the fact that we'd both had cheating husbands once upon a time. I'd used my divorce settlement for Donut Hearts, and she'd taken my cue and opened a shop of her own, this one following her own passion of feeding the birds. Unfortunately, she'd had trouble from the start with her business. Apparently there just hadn't been enough demand in April Springs for such a specialty shop, and she'd struggled from the beginning to make her monthly rent. Not only that, but once one of her clerks had been arrested for attempted murder. The best thing about For The Birds had been her discovering her birth mother was working beside her, so all in all, it hadn't *entirely* been a bad experience for her.

But it was all ending now, though we weren't letting her go out of business without a bang.

"That's odd. It shouldn't be locked," Jenny said with a frown. "Margaret was back there an hour ago, bringing out some of the last bits of stock that we haven't been able to move for ages. As far as I know, there are just a few boxes left, and then we'll be officially cleaned out."

"I thought you were calling her Mom these days," I said.

Jenny smiled slightly. "We finally decided that it would be Margaret at work and Mom everywhere else."

Trish Granger, owner of the Boxcar Grill, joined us. "Paige really needs that extension cord, Suzanne," she told us.

"It's one of the few things that's still *in* the storage room," Jenny said. "I'll go get it for you."

"You need to stay right where you are," I told her. "After all, this is your last hurrah. Don't worry. Trish and I can find it."

"If you can find the key," Jenny said as she rang up another sale. The day's event had transformed from a going-out-of-business sale to a chance for all of April Springs to get together and celebrate the hot late-summer day. The Fourth of July was long gone and Labor Day was just around the corner, and after a long and wet period of rain that seemed to have parked over us every day for weeks on end, people were using any excuse they could come up with for enjoying the lovely sunshine we were having at the moment.

"Don't worry. I'm sure *somebody* has it," Trish said. "Let me check with Grace. After all, she's taken this whole sale over."

"Since her company's covering our expenses, she can do whatever she wants to," Jenny said with a wry smile. "I still can't believe you're all pitching in for nothing."

"You'd do the same for any of us, and you know it," I told her.

"Absolutely," Trish echoed, "and besides, do you know how rare it is for me to be *outside* this time of day? I'm usually stuck behind the register at the Boxcar or waiting on tables."

Everyone knew how much she loved what she did, but that still didn't mean she couldn't complain a little about it, even if she didn't actually mean it.

"You don't have time to do this. You have to work your grill, and Suzanne, you're still selling donuts, aren't you?"

"Not anymore. We sold out," I told her proudly as I handed her a thick envelope. "This is all for you."

Jenny frowned a moment. "I kind of feel guilty taking this," she said.

"Maybe you do, but I'm pretty sure Gary Shook won't," I told her as I urged her to take the money.

Another cloud covered Jenny's face. "He's already been by twice, asking me when I was going to pay my final month's rent on the place. He's just awful."

"I know, but relish the fact that after today, you won't ever have to think of Gary Shook again," I told her.

"I guess it's true what they say about there being a silver lining to every dark cloud," she answered.

"Suzanne, you're going to find Paige an extension cord, right?" Trish asked me. "I really should get back to my grill."

"Go on. I'll be right there," I told her as Grace joined us.

"You've got quite a line of folks waiting for hamburgers and hot dogs," she told Trish.

"I'm on it," Trish said as she waved good-bye and made her way back to her grill.

"Do you happen to have the key to the storage room?" I asked Grace.

"No, but I didn't think it was locked," she said.

"How are we going to get that cord for Paige? She needs it for her cash register."

"If you jiggle the handle and push hard, you don't need a key," Jenny said as she made change for a woman I didn't recognize. We must have been drawing folks from out of town, which was no wonder given all that we were offering. Not only was Jenny selling out her stock at rock-bottom prices, but I'd been peddling donuts all morning, Paige was getting set up with her portable bookstore, Trish had switched from sausage-and-egg biscuits to hot dogs and hamburgers, and Grace had been handing out free samples of an absolutely garish shade of lipstick all morning.

"Come on, Suzanne. I'll help you break in," Grace said with a grin. "It's not going to be as much fun since we have the owner's permission, though."

"I'm just a renter, I'm not the owner, and I don't care a bit about Gary Shook's property," the shop owner said.

"Aren't you afraid you won't get your security deposit back?" I asked her.

Jenny just laughed. "Gary Shook has never returned a security deposit in his life. I have half a mind to punch a few holes in the walls on my way out just out of spite."

"I wouldn't do that if I were you, no matter how tempting it might be," I told her. "Knowing Shook, he'd probably take you to court."

"That's right, he's suing your mother, isn't he?" Jenny asked.

"Yes, it's some nuisance suit he filed because she beat him out of a deal," I said.

"That man makes enemies wherever he goes," Grace said. "Come on, Suzanne. Let's bust that door down."

"We're going to try to use a little finesse first though, right?" I asked her. I knew my best friend well enough to realize that she took great pleasure in the act of destruction. Subtlety had never exactly been her forte.

"Sure, but if we don't get it open on the second try, we're going to do it my way, right?"

"Fine," I said as we made our way through the nearly empty store to the back room. Most of the remaining merchandise had been moved out into the street to take advantage of the beautiful day, and I'd noticed a few confused birds trying to get seeds out of empty feeders hung from the trees around the strip mall where the shop was located.

As instructed, I jiggled the handle of the storeroom door and put a little pressure on the wood itself, but it wouldn't budge. "That's one," Grace said with a grin.

I tried again, this time putting my shoulder into it as I tried to twist the handle a little more forcefully. It resisted at first, and I heard Grace say over my shoulder, "Step aside, Suzanne, and let me give it a go."

Before I did that, I wanted to keep at it. Applying even more pressure, I practically threw myself against the door as I twisted the handle.

The flimsy door lock suddenly yielded to the pressure as the door flung open and nearly dumped me on the floor in the process.

I stumbled inside, fighting to keep my balance as I came face-to-face with something I'd hoped that I'd never see again in my life.

I was staring straight at a dead body, and worse yet, it was someone I knew.

Chapter 2

GARY SHOOK LAY THERE on the floor, his blank gaze staring upward at the ceiling. He might have been simply resting if it weren't for the small metal pole sticking out of his chest. The post was topped with a perpendicular rod extending out a foot toward his feet, and I knew exactly what it was. The pole's original use had been to hold a decorative yard flag, though this was a much beefier post than the ones I was used to. I knew what it was because Momma and Phillip still had one in the front yard of their cottage sporting a colorful image of fireworks from the Fourth of July.

"Suzanne, you nearly killed yourself on that door," Grace said as she hurried to help me up. Once she was inside, though, all her attention turned to the body. "That's Gary Shook! Is he ... dead?" she asked me.

I checked for a pulse, but I knew what I was going to find. There wasn't any life left in him. How long had he been back there, concealed behind a locked door? It surprised me that he'd gone undiscovered long enough to cool slightly, but how long did it really take for a person to become a body, anyway, especially with the air conditioning turned up to full blast? I'd had some experience with murder victims, but not enough to say one way or the other.

"There's no pulse, at least not that I can find, but we need Chief Grant," I ordered.

Stephen Grant was not only Grace's fiancé, he was also the chief of police for April Springs. I'd seen him ten minutes earlier patrolling the crowds that had been hovering around the front of the shop.

"I'll go grab him," she said as she stood. "Are you going to be okay here by yourself?" she asked me as she hesitated at the door.

"I'll be fine. Don't tell anyone what we found, would you? We don't want to set off a panic."

"I'm not going to have *any* trouble keeping my mouth shut about this," Grace said, and then she clearly had another thought. "How about Jenny? Should I say something to her?"

"Don't tell anyone," I repeated.

"Okay. Got it," Grace said, and then she was gone.

I stood and took in the scene, taking out my cell phone and snapping a handful of photos of the crime scene more out of habit than anything else. As I looked at Gary's body through my phone screen, I had to wonder who would do such a thing. Gary wasn't exactly beloved in our little town, but not liking someone and murdering him were two entirely different things. As Jenny had said, the storeroom was nearly empty of products, so that was something, anyway. Several empty shelves, a few errant boxes, and the extension cord we'd gone in search of were just about all that was there. I glanced in one of the boxes and found five more of the flag display stakes, so the murder weapon had been close at hand. That made me think that it had probably been done on impulse, at least given the use of that particular weapon.

That didn't necessarily mean that the murder hadn't been premeditated, though.

At least there was no doubt about it being intentional. There was no way Gary could have fallen onto that stake without bending it in the process. I knew those things were sharpened to a point. After all, they had to be in order to drive them into the dense clay soil we had in our part of North Carolina, but whoever had pushed it in hadn't stopped until they'd buried it a good four inches into the body. I knelt down and got a shot of just how deep it went into Gary's chest when I heard someone bark behind me. "What do you think you're doing, Suzanne?"

"I was just curious," I said as I stood to face our chief of police. He'd been a young man not all that long ago, but the job had clearly weighed on him since he'd taken it over, and now he was starting to show the signs of stress that he must have constantly been under.

"You didn't touch anything, did you?" he asked me as he knelt down.

"I know better than that," I said as I backed a few steps away.

"I know you do, but it doesn't hurt to confirm it," the chief said as he checked for a pulse himself. I didn't mind him doing it. In fact, I felt better knowing that no one was just going to take my word for it that the man was actually dead.

"Does this mean you have to shut the sale down?" I asked him as he studied the body.

"What do you think?" he asked me. "This is clearly a homicide. I really don't have much choice."

"Maybe you should rethink that for a second," I suggested as he called for the paramedics outside on his radio.

"Why should I do that?" he asked me.

"Chief, you can seal off this room, even the shop, but do you really want to disperse the crowd, which could very well still include the killer?" I asked him.

"Suzanne, I can't just act as though nothing happened here," he said sternly.

"No one is asking you to do that, but would it hurt to send a few men out with cameras to take pictures of the crowd so you at least have an idea of who's there? The longer you can sit on this, the better chance you have of catching someone off guard."

"What you're not saying is that it would help Jenny out, too," he said calmly.

"Really? The thought never even crossed my mind," I said with a shrug.

"Liar," the chief said with the hint of a smile. "Okay, I'll think about it. Now kindly leave me to my crime scene, would you?"

"I'm more than happy to oblige," I said as I walked out of the store-room. Two paramedics hurried past me as I headed out of the shop, and Jenny was taking it all in.

"What's happening back there, Suzanne?" she asked, the concern thick in her voice. "Are you okay?"

"I'm perfectly fine," I said.

"Well, *something's* going on," she replied. "I know for a fact that there's *nothing* all that interesting back there."

"When was the last time you were back there yourself?" I asked her.

"I don't know, maybe an hour ago, right around the time Margaret was there," she said oddly. "Why?"

"Was she the last one there, or were you?" I asked.

"I couldn't tell you," Jenny admitted. "Things have been so crazy that this entire day is just one big blur. Is it important?"

I didn't want to tell her what I'd found, but she'd learn the truth soon enough, and I would rather she found out from me than from seeing them take the body away. Plus, Chief Grant hadn't exactly prohibited me from telling anyone about our discovery.

"It's Gary Shook," I said.

"What's Gary Shook?" she asked me.

"You need to keep your cool when I tell you. Promise me you'll do that, Jenny."

"What did he do, make a pass at you, *too*? He's a bug, and somebody needs to step on him once and for all."

"You don't have to worry about Gary anymore," I told her softly. "He's dead."

I wasn't sure what I thought her reaction was going to be, but it was still odd when her face went white and she said, "I can't believe it. Now I'm going to go to jail for the rest of my life."

Was that a confession, or was it something else entirely? Either way, I was glad that our police chief hadn't heard that particular statement from a woman who apparently had every reason in the world to want to see the victim dead, had the means, and had had a golden opportunity as well.

I didn't exactly have to catch Jenny to keep her from falling, but she did stumble back against the building where she'd placed her register outside. At least no one else was around at that moment, so I was the only one who'd heard her statement. "What are you talking about, Jenny? Did you kill him?" I asked her softly. I hadn't *had* to ask that question, but I wanted to know nonetheless. Besides, given what she'd just told me, it was a fair query.

"No, but I threatened him in public this morning, and if he's dead now, who do you think the police are going to come looking for?" she asked as she stood there in shock.

"Jenny, all you did was *threaten* him, though, right?"

"Yes," she said woodenly, and then the magnitude of what I'd said got her attention. "Suzanne, *I* certainly didn't kill him."

"I understand that, but it doesn't look good you acting guilty and making statements that might make folks think that you had something to do with it," I explained as Grace walked up, her frown intense.

"Why are you out here? What's going on?" she asked me as she glanced back to the storeroom.

"The chief's back there, along with a couple of paramedics," I told her. Grace glanced over at Jenny, so I added, "It's okay. She knows."

"I'm kind of in shock, I think," Jenny said.

"Join the club," Grace answered, and then she turned to me. "Suzanne, are we going to have to shut it all down?"

"I asked the chief to let us keep everything open, and he's thinking about it," I said. "Speaking of which, we need to take some pictures of the crowd in case whoever did it is waiting around for us to discover the body."

"Who would do such a thing?" Jenny asked us softly.

"You'd be surprised," I answered.

Grace nodded. "I thought of the same thing. That's what took me so long to get back here. I've been milling around, getting some shots of the crowd for the last five minutes."

"Great minds think alike, I guess," I said with a nod of approval.

"Where's Jake, Suzanne? Should you give him a call?" Jenny asked me.

"He's in Raleigh working on a case," I told her. My husband, Jake Bishop, had left the day before so he could take a case and spend some time with his sister and her kids. It honestly wouldn't have surprised me if that hadn't been why he'd taken the case to begin with. Jake was a good man with a big heart, and given his sister's propensity to date less-than-ideal men, he was constantly being pulled toward her and his niece and nephew. I didn't begrudge him the trip or the job, though. Jake had even offered me a chance to tag along with him again, but I'd quickly declined. The bad taste of our last trip together was still in my mouth, and I figured it would be quite some time before I took him up on an offer like that again.

"Okay." Jenny seemed to be in some kind of trance, but after a moment, she snapped out of it. "Will the two of *you* help me?"

"What do you need us to do?" I asked her. "This is all about to wind down anyway, but we'll pitch in any way we can."

"I'm not talking about the sale, and you know it. I need you two to find out who really killed Gary Shook in my shop," she said. "If you don't, I know I'm going to go to jail, and I didn't kill him!" The last part was said a bit shrilly, not that I could blame her. I knew from firsthand experience that it wasn't great being a suspect in a murder case, and I hoped that I'd never have to experience that again.

I was about to answer her when Chief Grant came out looking rather grim, which wasn't that big a surprise given the circumstances. I had to wonder if he'd made up his mind on whether he was shutting down the sale after all, but if he had, I was going to do my best to argue him out of it. After all, every penny we brought in for Jenny would go toward her getting away from this store—and her decision to open it—once and forever, and at the moment that was our priority, not finding a killer.

"Are you shutting us down?" I asked him as he approached.

"No, at least not yet," the chief said. Then he turned to Jenny. "We need to talk."

"I didn't do it!" she protested loudly.

"Take it easy," Chief Grant said, trying his best to keep her calm. "Nobody's accusing you of anything, at least not yet. When was the last time you were in your storeroom?"

"About an hour ago," Jenny said.

"Did anyone go with you?" he asked.

"No, I went in alone. Margaret went in about the same time I did, but I can't remember which of us was the last one to leave. She had an errand to run, so I was holding down the fort here alone. I grabbed a few things and then went back out front."

"Can anyone get back there without you knowing it?" he asked. It was a great question, and I was surprised that I hadn't thought to ask it myself.

"There's a back door in the corner behind some boxes, but it's always locked," she said.

The police chief disappeared and then came back a few minutes later. "It's not locked now," he answered. "Who all has a key?"

"Just me," she said sullenly.

"Surely Gary had one, too," I piped up.

"Of course he did," Jenny answered.

"So, that's how you think Gary got in without anyone seeing him?" Grace asked her fiancé.

"I'm not speculating on anything at the moment," the chief answered her. "I'm just trying to gather information." He smiled softly as he added that last bit. I knew that he had to dance a fine line when he was speaking to Grace in his official capacity, since Jake had done the same thing with me in the past when *he'd* been our police chief.

"Got it," she said.

"I notice you have two security cameras in the store," the chief said, continuing his questioning of Jenny. If he minded us being there, he didn't say so, and I wasn't about to volunteer to leave until I was ordered to.

"I'm afraid they won't do you any good. They've been dead for a few months," she answered glumly.

"I didn't think they let you cancel those contracts without some pretty severe penalties," the chief noted.

"I didn't either, but it's a fact that when you stop paying them, they kill their services pretty quickly," she replied.

"So we don't have *any* record of who came in or out of your shop today, either through the front door or the one in back," he said with a frown.

"Sorry. I wish I had better news, but there's nothing I can do about it. Please don't shut us down, Chief."

"I'm not, at least not for the moment at any rate," Chief Grant said. He looked around the shop. "It looks as though you've been pretty much cleaned out, anyway."

"There are still things for sale outside, and that doesn't include the fundraisers my friends are holding for me," Jenny said. "I'd appreciate it if you could let us finish."

"I can't make any promises. Besides, we're going to be bringing the body out soon, and I doubt *anyone* is going to want anything, especially food, after they see that. How long do you think it might take to wrap things up here?" the chief asked him.

"Suzanne?" Jenny asked me. "You'd know that better than I would."

"My donuts are gone, but Paige hasn't even finished setting up her sales table for her books yet. I'd say Trish is halfway through with her food vending. Grace, how are you doing? Have you met the requirements you needed to sponsor this thing?"

"I don't have a sample left, so we're good on that front," she said. "It's amazing how quickly folks will take something when it's free."

I'd given away my fair share of unsold donuts in the past, so she wasn't telling me anything that I didn't already know. "It's obviously your call. What would you like us to do, Chief?"

Chief Grant seemed surprised that I was asking him his preference, but I felt as though I at least owed him that much. "Tell you what. Once my people finish up out there," he said with a knowing look in my direction, "the sooner we end this the better, at least as far as I'm concerned."

I knew he was talking about taking photos of the crowd still present. I didn't tell him that Grace had already thought of doing that. We'd tell him soon enough, but right now, we had other things to address. "How about this? If we move Trish and Paige to the donut shop, we could keep this thing going," I suggested. "We could even move the rest of your stock and set all of it up in front of Donut Hearts."

"You'd do that for me?" Jenny asked.

"You bet we would," I answered. "What do you think, Grace? Can we make it happen?"

"Let's move this party!" Grace agreed enthusiastically. "I'll go help Paige."

"And I'll see if Trish needs a hand," I added.

"What should I do?" Jenny asked.

"Stay close. We have more to talk about," Chief Grant said.

"Should we hang around in case you need us?" I asked Jenny as I lingered a bit.

At that moment, Margaret came rushing forward, clearly out of breath and upset about something. No doubt she'd heard about us finding Gary Shook's body in the back of the shop. The truth was that it wouldn't have surprised me if everyone in town already knew what had happened. Margaret hugged her birth daughter and temporary employer. "You're not going to jail for this, Jenny. I won't let it happen."

"Nobody's going to jail, Mom," Jenny said softly as she broke free of her.

"That's the spirit," she said. "Chief, if you're intent on arresting someone, it should be me, not my daughter."

Chief Grant frowned at the older woman. "Why, did *you* kill the man, Margaret?"

"What? No, of course not, but neither did my daughter. But if you're looking for a scapegoat, let it be me. I've lived a full and happy life. I'm willing to sacrifice my freedom for my daughter's happiness."

"That's not the way it works," he said with a frown. "And just for the record, I don't appreciate you implying that I'd frame someone for a murder they didn't commit just to clear a case off the books, either."

That admission caught Margaret by surprise. "I'm so sorry, Stephen. I didn't mean to imply that you weren't good at your job. Please forgive me."

The chief studied her for a few seconds before nodding. "You're forgiven." He then turned back to Jenny. "Now, why don't you follow me back inside?"

"She's not going anywhere without me," Margaret said adamantly.

"I'm okay with that for now as long as you stay out of my way," the chief answered.

After the three of them walked back inside the wild bird supply shop, Grace asked with a grin, "Would *you* confess to a crime you didn't commit to save *me*, Suzanne?"

"If I have the choice, I'd rather prove that you were innocent," I said with a shrug.

"But if push came to shove?"

"Sure, why not? How about you?"

"Are you kidding? I love you like a sister, but I'm not going to jail for anybody!"

We both laughed at her over-the-top performance as we split up and went our separate ways. Even though Grace had denied it, I *knew* that she'd give her life up for me, and she knew that I'd do the same for her. It was a point of pride and satisfaction for me that in a world that was full of continuing troubles, I could always count on Grace. In fact, I had a support group that rivaled any I'd ever heard of. There was Jake, my mother, her husband, Trish, Paige, and half a dozen more friends besides Grace that I knew I could count on when things got tough. If the number of people I could count on in a pinch were gold, I'd be rich beyond all dreams of avarice.

The truth was that in every way that mattered, I was a very wealthy woman. When the chips were down, a fat bank balance couldn't do a thing to keep my spirits up, and any friends I might try to buy would be worth less than they cost me.

No, what I had was the real thing, solid gold in every way that mattered.

Chapter 3

"TRISH, CAN WE MOVE your grill over to the donut shop?" I asked her as she finished selling two hamburgers to Jackson Boles, a steady customer of hers at the Boxcar Grill.

"What's wrong with staying right here where we are?" she asked me as she waited on her next customer.

"We've decided to move everything to Springs Drive between the Boxcar and Donut Hearts," I said, not wanting to get into the reasons why. Apparently everyone in town hadn't heard about the murder, at least not yet, but that would surely change soon enough, and I wanted to be in our new location when that happened. "Can you do it?"

"Of course I can. All I need is for the mayor to fetch his new tractor back here, hook my grill up to it, and then haul it back to where it needs to be. That's how we got it here in the first place, but I need to sell out what I've got on the grill first."

I looked and saw that there were half a dozen hamburgers left and nearly a dozen hot dogs still on the grill. "How long do you think that will take?"

"No more than five or ten minutes, which should be long enough for you to get George Morris and have him come over. He's riding that tractor around town as though he's a one-man parade," she said with a grin. "I'm surprised he doesn't have a campaign poster on each side of the thing."

"Him being out and about on it is probably enough advertisement enough," I answered. "I'll be right back."

Three minutes later, I found George pulled over in the shade, not sitting on his tractor at all but instead keeping company with a dear friend of mine. "Angelica, how did you get away from Napoli's in the middle of the lunch rush?" I asked her.

Angelica DeAngelis was a beautiful woman on any given day, but when she smiled, it was almost painful to take in her loveliness. "I wanted to see your mayor out and about with his new pride and joy." The owner of Napoli's, Union Square's finest and only Italian restaurant, had been dating George for some time now, and I for one was thrilled to see that they were still together.

George grinned at her. "That's just a tractor, and no matter how pretty and shiny it might be, there's something else that's caught my eye these days, something quite a bit more important to me."

Angelica actually blushed a bit from the compliment. "You are too smooth for your own good, Mr. Mayor," she said with a smile.

"George? Smooth? I don't think so," I answered good-naturedly, though it was true my old friend had come even more out of his shell since he'd begun dating Angelica.

"You'd be surprised," Angelica said as she leaned over and kissed his cheek. It was now the mayor's turn to blush, something that was an odd sight for me to see. "Farewell, my friends," she said with a wave of her hand.

"I'll see you tomorrow night, Angel," George said as he walked with her a few paces.

"I will count the hours," she answered.

Once she was gone, I caught the mayor looking wistfully after her. "She's pretty amazing, isn't she?" I asked, though I already knew the answer.

"In more ways than I can count," he answered. "What are you doing out roaming around? Don't tell me you already sold out of donuts."

"I did, but that's not why I'm here. We need you to tow Trish's grill to the front of Donut Hearts on the double."

"Why, has she sold out, too?" he asked.

"No, but we're relocating the sale," I answered.

"Why on earth would you want to do that?" George asked me, clearly puzzled by my statement.

"You haven't heard the news, have you?" How had the police chief not told the mayor yet?

"Heard what?"

"Someone stabbed and killed Gary Shook in the heart in the For The Birds store room," I said.

The smile vanished from George's face in an instant. "Let's go," he said as he headed in the direction of the closing shop, temporarily abandoning his shiny red toy right where it was.

"We need you and your tractor, Mr. Mayor," I reminded him.

"Suzanne, a man has died. That takes precedence over a going-out-of-business sale," he said sternly.

"George, I hate to be the one to tell you this, but you're not a cop anymore. Chief Grant and his crew are investigating the murder. We need you, as the mayor, to upset as few folks as possible. That's why we're moving everything over to the park."

"You need me for my tractor, you mean," he corrected me.

"Maybe so, but not *just* for your tractor," I replied. "You are a calming influence around here, and we're going to need *all* of your skills before the day is out."

He seemed to get a little bit smaller as he nodded. "You're right. Come on, let's go move that grill. Want a ride?"

"On the fender?" I asked as I looked at the precarious perch. "No thanks, it looks too dangerous. I think I'd rather walk."

"The truth is that you'll probably still beat me there," George allowed.

"I'll keep you company and walk beside you then," I said.

"You're just in time," Trish said as George started to back the tractor up to the trailer hitch of the large steel grill. It had to be on wheels, because I couldn't imagine anyone moving it otherwise with anything short of a crane. "I just sold out that batch of food."

"How did you manage to do it so quickly?" I asked her.

"What can I say? I was motivated," she answered.

Once George had the grill hooked up, he started toward my shop with Trish walking beside him.

"I'll see you over there," I told them. "I want to check on Paige."

"We'll be there and set up again in no time," Trish said with a grin. "Well, maybe not no time, but before sunset anyway."

"It's your choice. Do you want me to go fast, or do you want to keep your grill on its wheels?" he asked her.

"You're doing fine just the way you're going now, Mayor," she answered him with a slight grin.

Since they were set, I headed over to Paige's table. Unfortunately, she hadn't even begun to pack since Grace had gone to see her, and I wondered just what the problem might be.

One thing was sure; I was about to find out.

"What's the holdup?" I asked Paige and Grace.

"We're just waiting on transportation," Paige said.

"Sorry for the confusion," I told her. "I know it's a real hassle hauling everything back to Springs Drive after bringing it over here."

"What can you do? Nobody planned for a murder," Paige said with a sad grin. "I don't like saying it, but I don't envy the police chief figuring out who might have done it. Gary made more than his share of enemies around here in the last six months."

"I know he did," I said.

"Where did he come from originally?" Grace asked me.

"He grew up in Union Square," I said.

"What I want to know is where he got all of that money," Paige replied.

"I've heard a few different stories," I said. "One rumor was that he inherited a load of cash from a rich aunt and decided to get involved in real estate."

"If that were true, why would he come to April Springs to start his little one-man empire?" Grace asked me.

"I heard it was part of a codicil in the woman's will," I said. "She knew he'd burned quite a few bridges in Union Square, so she wanted him to get a fresh start somewhere else." It was amazing the amount of minutiae I picked up selling donuts and keeping my eyes and ears open.

"Okay, what else have you heard?" Paige asked me.

"Well, another story claims that he won a wad of cash in a poker game, and he had to find a way to launder it without paying taxes on it, so he decided to come here to lie low."

"I can't see Gary Shook being a gambler, can you?" Paige asked me.

"Did you know him very well?" I asked her. There had been something about the way she'd posed the question that made me think there was more going on behind the scenes than I knew.

"No, not really," she said, blushing slightly at the confession.

Grace caught onto it as quickly as I did. "You didn't actually *date* that man, did you?" she asked with a laugh.

"It wasn't my proudest moment, so I'd appreciate it if you didn't get so much joy out of my error in judgment," Paige said a little stiffly.

Grace apologized immediately. "I'm so sorry; that was out of line. Goodness knows I've made more than *my* share of mistakes in the past. Far be it from me to have fun at your expense because of one of yours. Would it help if I told you some of the humiliating things I've done myself?" she offered.

Paige's stern look softened instantly. "No, we're good. Anyway, Gary Shook could be really charming when he wanted to be."

"He just must not have wanted to be that way all that often," I said.

Paige and Grace both looked at me oddly. "Suzanne, do *you* have something you want to tell us?" Grace asked.

"Of course not," I said quickly. "I would never cheat on Jake, but if I did, do you honestly think it would be with *Gary Shook*?" I turned to Paige and added, "Not that there's anything wrong with anyone who might have dated him."

"Oh, there was plenty of things wrong with it," she said ruefully. "Why did you have a problem with him, Suzanne?"

"He and Momma were sort of rivals in business," I said. "He tried to bully her into backing down from a deal a few months ago."

Grace grinned. "He didn't dare."

"He most certainly did," I confirmed.

"The man was absolutely suicidal to try something like that," Grace said.

"Maybe so, but there was nothing self-inflicted in that double chest wound," I answered, thinking about what I'd nearly tumbled onto when I'd opened that door.

"A double wound?" Paige asked. "Someone actually stabbed him twice?"

"No, but those lawn flagpoles have *two* sharp points on them," I explained. "They are only about four inches long, but obviously that was more than enough to be lethal."

"I would think so," Paige said with a shiver. "I wasn't a fan of the man, but I doubt he deserved that even with the way he treated me, Jenny, *and* his other renters." She hesitated before adding, "Chief Grant doesn't think that she did it, does he?"

"Who knows what he's thinking?" Grace asked quickly. It was obvious she didn't want to speculate as to her fiancé's reasoning, and I couldn't blame her. When Jake was detecting, I did my best to respect his right to investigate without my input.

Well, mostly, anyway.

"Here comes my crack team of movers now," Paige said as two pickup trucks approached in single file. One truck had probably looked abandoned at least twenty years earlier, and it appeared that the rust on the frame was being held together with nothing more than wishful thinking. It had been painted several different colors over the years, a not-all-that-unpleasing blend of tones and hues, and it looked as though it belonged to an aging hippy, which it most certainly did.

Gladiola Jones got out, her long gray hair braided and hanging down past her bibbed overalls, which sported more paint samples than her truck. She wore sandals made of old car tires, and she sported a woven straw hat that I was sure she'd crafted herself. Gladiola was a true child of the sixties, and she still obviously continued the lifestyle even after she'd become a grandmother.

Speaking of grandchildren, one of hers followed her in a truck of his very own. They appeared to be about the same make and model, but Jim's truck was waxed and polished within an inch of its life. Jim must have recently passed his driver's test, because he was behind the wheel with his nervous father JT sitting beside him. JT wouldn't tell anyone his real name, but Gladiola was proud to tell anyone who asked that it was Juniper Thrush. JT was an accountant in town, and though he gave his mother grief whenever I saw them together, he clearly loved her dearly.

Gladiola got out of her truck, hugged her grandson, and then gave her son a peck on the cheek. "Nice wheels, Bub."

"Thanks, Gran," he said with a grin.

"That thing has so many coats of wax on it that if he ever hits anybody, he'll just slide right off," JT said. "Why are you moving your booth so soon, Paige?"

"Circumstances beyond my control," the bookseller said. As we loaded boxes, tables, and the register into the trucks, she added, "Thanks for coming back so quickly."

"Are you kidding? I can't get him out of this thing," JT said proudly of his son. He added softly, "We spent a year restoring it together in our garage, and I'm not ashamed to say that it was the best year of my life."

"He's a good kid," I said.

"He's a good man," JT gently corrected me.

"They grow up fast, don't they?" I asked.

"Too fast for my taste," he added wistfully.

"Are you two going to stand there gabbing all day, or are you going to get some work done?" Gladiola asked us with a grin. "After all, you can't expect us young people to do everything."

"My mother is seventy-four years old, and she thinks she's middle-aged," JT said with mock severity.

"Hey, it's important to have a goal, and mine's to hit an even one hundred and forty-eight," Gladiola said as she patted her son's cheek affectionately. "Besides, what are you going to do with yourself when I'm gone?"

"I'll be lost without you, and you know it," JT said earnestly.

"No worries, Sport. I'm not planning on going anywhere for a very long time."

"We don't always get what we want though," I said.

Gladiola looked toward For The Birds. "We heard what happened," she answered somberly. She shook her head abruptly as though she was trying to rid herself of a pesky gnat to clear away the dark thoughts. "That should do it," she said as she loaded the last box into her truck. "Is the caravan ready to roll?"

"We'll be right behind you," Paige said.

"Ride with me, Sunshine," Gladiola said. "You've never been in Ty before."

"You named your truck Ty?" I asked her.

"It's short for tie-dye," JT said with a grin.

"Don't pay him any mind," she said as she stroked her truck's hood and spoke gently to it. "He's just jealous that *you're* my favorite."

JT laughed despite his attempt at looking stern earlier. "Come on, Mom. Let's go."

She nodded. "Do you want to lead this train, Jim?"

"You bet I do," the young man said enthusiastically.

"The speed limit is twenty-five through here," JT reminded his son.

"You worry too much, Pops," Jim said with a grin.

"Pops? I love it," Gladiola said with a grin. She put her arm around her son's shoulder and said, "Come on, Pops. Let's go."

"What am I going to do with the two of you?" he asked as he shook his head.

"Enjoy us while you can," Gladiola said.

"That's what I'm trying to do," he said.

"How about you two? Want to hitch a ride in the back of my truck?" Gladiola asked us. "I've got room if you're not squeamish about airbags and seat belts."

"Thanks, but we'll walk over. It's not that far," I said.

"Sissies," Gladiola said with a smile. "Come on, Paige. Let's show them how it's done."

The bookstore owner looked at us both askance as she got into Gladiola's truck, but there was nothing we could do to help her.

After the trucks were gone and most of the other folks had migrated to Springs Drive and Donut Hearts in particular, I glanced back at For The Birds.

They must have snuck a stretcher into the shop while I'd been away, because I saw the paramedics carting off a large shape in a body bag. No doubt Gary Shook was on his way to the morgue.

I was about to say something to Grace about heading over to Donut Hearts when I saw Chief Grant come out of the store as well.

He waved us over to him, and Grace and I immediately changed directions to see what the chief had to say to us.

Chapter 4

"WHERE'S JENNY?" I ASKED him before he had a chance to say a word.

"I didn't arrest her, Suzanne, or Margaret either, for that matter. I'm still just trying to figure out what happened." His tone was defensive, and I knew that I'd pushed him too hard earlier.

"Hey, Margaret really wasn't accusing you of anything before, Stephen," Grace said gently. "She was just upset about the murder. I am too, as a matter of fact."

"Sorry," he said as he offered a hint of a smile. "I guess I'm just a bit touchy at the moment. Gabby Williams just left here."

"What was Gabby doing here?" I asked him. Her shop, ReNEWed, was in limbo at the moment after problems with the rebuild that were ongoing. I'd been under the impression that Gabby was leaving town for a while to clear her head, but evidently she was back now.

"She went to great lengths to tell me not to rush to judgment on Jenny's guilt or innocence," he explained. "You know she and Margaret go way back."

"I did know that, as a matter of fact," I said. "You can't blame her for looking out for her friend's kid, Chief."

"I just wish everyone would trust me to do my job," he replied, clearly a bit frustrated by all of the meddling that went on in April Springs.

"Including us?" Grace asked him with the hint of a smile.

"I'd be lying if I tried to deny it," he answered with a touch of humor himself.

"I'm truly sorry about that, but you know we're going to help Jenny. We don't feel as though we have any choice," I said.

"Knowing it and liking it are two different things," the chief said. "Have you two Nosy Rosies figured anything out yet?"

I wasn't about to chide him for asking us for our input. As long as we cooperated with him, he managed to tolerate us, which was something we needed from whoever was the current chief of police. "I got some photos with my phone of the crime scene, but I'm sure your people got better ones."

"I took photos of the crowd," Grace offered.

"He had his people doing that, too," I offered.

"Hang on. That doesn't mean that I don't want to see what you've both got," he said. "Forward them to me, would you?"

"Me, too," I said.

"Send yours to me as well." Grace pulled out her phone, and a few seconds later, mine pinged that I had incoming email. She worked that phone like fisherman handled a rod and reel, but then again, in her business, it was kind of crucial.

The file was a big one, so I'd have to look through it later. It took me a bit longer to load my photos, but I managed it somehow. In the meantime, I realized that we, or more precisely I, had interrupted the police chief before he'd had a chance to say anything.

"Sorry, I didn't mean to interrupt you earlier," I told him. "Were you about to say something?"

"I just wanted to tell Grace that I probably won't be able to make it for dinner tonight like we'd planned," he told her sheepishly.

She took a few steps forward and kissed him on the cheek. "Don't worry, I understand completely. Since Jake is out of town, I'm sure Suzanne and I will find *something* to eat."

"There's no doubt in my mind about that," he said with a smile.

"Hey, was that a dig?" I asked him, happy to see even a brief moment of happiness from the young man.

"It might have been, but was he wrong, Suzanne?" Grace asked me.

"I never said that," I answered.

"As much as I'd love to stay and chat with you ladies, I've got work to do," the chief answered, the lightness in him gone as quickly as it had come.

Chief Grant headed back into the shop, and I looked at Grace as she watched him. A frown had creased her lips.

"Hey, is everything okay? You're not really that upset about dinner, are you?" I asked her.

"What? No, of course not. I'm worried about him, Suzanne. He takes these things much too personally, and I'm afraid of what it's doing to him."

"He'll be okay," I said, doing my best to buoy her spirits.

"Do you really think so, or are you just saying that to make me feel better?" she asked me as she glanced in my direction.

"Can't it be a little of both?" I asked her. "Either way, we can't do anything about it. Come on, let's go to see how things are going in front of the donut shop."

"We might as well," Grace answered. It was clear that her thoughts were going to be with her fiancé, which was as it should be, but maybe I'd be able to distract her with the rest of our efforts to break Jenny away from the debts of her defunct shop.

As we walked toward Springs Drive, I said, "If you'd rather we didn't, we don't *have* to help Jenny with this case, you know."

"I don't see it that way. She asked us for our help, and we agreed. We can't just go back on our word," Grace answered promptly.

"I understand that," I reminded her. "But if it will help make things better between you and Stephen, I can get someone else to give me a hand."

"Thanks for the offer, but I'm on the team, no discussion allowed."

"Yes, ma'am," I said with a nod. "Gosh, I forgot just how forceful you could be when you wanted something."

"How is that even possible?" Grace asked me with a sly grin.

"I don't know. I must have been distracted for a second there," I told her. "So, we're going forward with our plan to help Jenny, but that doesn't mean we have to be that obvious about it. For now, we'll keep our inquiries discreet as long as we can."

"I can do subtle," Grace agreed.

"All evidence to the contrary," I added.

"Was it absolutely necessary to add that last bit?" she asked me.

"Maybe not necessary, but true nonetheless," I said with a laugh.

"That's fair," she answered. "It looks like most of the crowd has come over," Grace added as we hit Springs Drive near the town clock. Folks were milling about the tables Paige had just set up and were already buying books at a reduced price. She was really coming through for Jenny, and so was Trish, too. She'd put another round of burgers and hot dogs on the grill, and I saw the mayor sitting on his tractor in the shade with one of each in his hands.

"Are those for us?" I asked him mockingly as I reached out for his food.

"Sorry. These are the first installment of my moving fees," he said with a grin, and then he took a big bite of his hot dog, getting mustard on his chin in the process. I decided the penalty for not sharing his food was not telling him what we'd learned, and when Grace started to say something, I shook her off.

"You're really charging her?" I asked. "This is for Jenny, remember?"

"Hey, I've got to at least recoup my gas," he protested.

"You're kidding, right?" I asked him again.

"Of course I'm kidding. I bought both of these, and if you're nice to me, I might just buy a hot dog for each one of you."

"Thanks, but we can pay our own way," I said.

"Hey, I was just joking," George answered.

"So was Suzanne," Grace said. "How much are the dogs and burgers?"

"Hot dogs are a buck and hamburgers are two," he said as he reached for his wallet. "Sorry, all I've got is a ten."

"That'll do just fine," Grace said with a grin.

"Any chance I'll get change back from that?" he asked her as she headed for the grill.

"Maybe a little, but I wouldn't count on it. It's for a good cause, remember?"

"I do," he said with a shrug. "Oh, well. Easy come, easy go," he told me after Grace got in line with his money. "That was nice of you all to do this for Jenny," the mayor said.

"We'd have done the same for anybody else," I said.

"Maybe, maybe not."

"What do you mean?"

"Haven't you heard? Gary Shook has been going around raising the rents on *all* of his properties for the past few days. There are half a dozen folks who are going to have to shut their businesses down because of the rent hikes, not just Jenny."

"Will they still have to move now?" I asked. It hadn't even occurred to me that Gary had bumped up his rent for more than just Jenny, but it made sense. After all, in for a penny, in for a pound.

"That's a fair question. Until his estate goes through probate, I'm guessing that the executor will leave things exactly the way they are right now. That's what I'd do if I were in charge of it, anyway."

"Do you have any idea who that might be?" I asked him. The mayor had more connections in April Springs than I could ever dream of having, and if anyone would know, he would be the one.

"No, but I can ask around if it's important to you," he offered. "If I find anything out, I'll let you know. Otherwise, if it's quiet on my end, it means I couldn't come up with an answer for you."

"That's good enough for me. Thanks." Almost as an afterthought, I said, "Don't let anyone know who's asking, okay?"

"Got it," he said with a nod. "Are you trying to keep a low profile on this one?"

"That's our hope. Why aren't you surprised that Grace and I are going to dig into this?"

"The truth is that I would be surprised if you weren't," he answered.

"Are we really getting that predictable?" I asked him.

"Maybe not to most folks, but we go back a long ways, Suzanne. Once upon a time, we worked together solving murders around here, remember?"

"I'm not likely to forget," I told him, remembering the accident—or intended murder more appropriately—that had nearly killed him, all at my behest.

"Hey, I'm not some feeble old man. If you need me, all you have to do is ask."

"I will," I said as Grace came up with a tray overflowing with two hot dogs, two hamburgers, and two sodas.

"That looks good," George said.

"I'm betting it will be. Thanks for lunch, Mr. Mayor," Grace said as she handed me the tray and hugged the mayor.

"Was I right before? There's not going to be any change, is there?"

"Nope, I put what was left in the tip jar," she said with a grin. "Who knew you were such a generous sweetie pie?"

"Let's not spread that particular rumor around," he told us. "If you both don't mind sitting on my lap, you could join me on my tractor."

There was no way on earth the three of us would fit onto that tiny seat. "Thanks for the offer, but I think we'll eat over there," I told him. "If we tried to sit with you, people would talk."

"It might hurt your reputations, but it would do wonders for mine," George said with a grin.

"Haven't you got enough on your hands with Angelica?" Grace asked him.

"More than I can handle, truth be told," he answered with a grin. "But so far, it's been a blast trying."

"I bet," I said. "Thanks again for lunch."

"It was my pleasure," he said as we walked toward a free bench in the park.

"Are we really letting him buy us lunch?" I asked her.

Grace grinned at me. "When I hugged him, I slipped a twenty into his pocket. It was worth every penny of it getting the chance to tease him."

I pulled out a ten of my own and handed it to her. "I want to go in halfsies with you."

"I won't say no and deprive you of the right to join in the fun," she answered as she took my money and then had a bite of her burger. "Man, these are even better grilled out, aren't they?"

"I think so," I said as I took a bite of my hot dog. As we ate, we watched folks wander around the park, and I noticed one of them carrying one of the heavy-duty garden flagpoles identical to the one that had skewered Gary Shook. "It's hard to believe that could actually kill someone."

"They're pretty sturdy, even if they are only a few feet tall," she said. "When do we start investigating?"

I looked at my watch. "We've got to stay here and help out with this sale for another few hours, so after we clean up, I say we get started. Are you *sure* you want to do this?"

"I'm positive," she said as Momma and her husband, former chief of police Phillip Martin, walked over to join us.

"Can you believe what happened to Gary Shook?" Phillip asked as he neared us.

"Phillip, they are the ones who found the body. Of *course* they can believe it," Momma said sternly to her husband. "I didn't think we were going to talk about it."

"Come on, Dot, how can we not? We're living in some crazy times these days."

"I hardly think one more homicide in April Springs qualifies as all that unusual as of late," my mother corrected him.

I had to agree with Phillip. "One more is one too many as far as I'm concerned, too," I told them.

"See? She's on *my* side," my stepfather crowed.

"She most certainly isn't," Momma said. "Tell him, Suzanne."

"The truth is that I think you're both pretty," I said. It was my standard answer when two people were trying to drag me into an argument that I had no business being anywhere close to.

"Suzanne," Momma said curtly, scolding me instead of her husband. I wasn't exactly sure that I liked that any better.

"What I meant to say was that you both present valid points of view," I answered quickly.

"You're digging into this case, aren't you?" Phillip asked me. "How can you not? Of course you are."

"My daughter doesn't need to involve herself in *every* homicide that occurs within a thirty-mile radius of April Springs, Phillip," Momma said.

I hated to do it, but I couldn't keep the truth from them. "I'm sorry, but this one I do. Jenny asked us for our help, and I don't know how we could have said no, given the circumstances," I explained.

Momma frowned for a moment before answering. Sometimes it was easy to forget just how diminutive she was, her personality was so much bigger than life. "Must you?"

"You're the one who taught me never to break my word once I give it," I reminded her. It was a risky move using my mother's own parenting skills against her, but I wasn't sure what else I could say that would have as much impact.

"That's certainly true enough," she answered finally with a bit of a sigh. "Well, if you must do it, I hope you two will at least be careful."

"We always are, Dot," Grace said.

"I expect you to look after my daughter, young lady," Momma told my best friend sternly.

"Yes, ma'am," Grace answered as though we were kids again.

"And Suzanne, you need to do the same for Grace," she continued.

"I *always* do," I answered, and when I realized she wasn't all that thrilled with my flippant tone of voice, I quickly added, "But I promise that I will do my best."

"Make sure that it is your *very* best," Momma said.

"I will," I answered. "Momma, you didn't get along with Gary Shook, did you?"

"He was a pest, a gnat flying around me in need of a good swatting," Momma said concisely.

"Don't hold back, Dot. Tell us how you really feel," Grace told her with a grin.

"Ladies, I refuse to lie about someone's character, or lack thereof, just because they're dead. He threatened me with two nuisance lawsuits in the past three weeks that he knew that he had no hope of winning. His goal was to try to embarrass me, to bully me, and to make me back down from a deal I'd entered into that he'd been trying to get for himself for a month."

"So it's really true? Someone tried to bully *you*?" Grace asked her. "Boy, talk about knowing your audience. Only someone who didn't know you would try to do that, Dot."

If I had said it, I would have gotten the glare to end all glares, but she took it in stride since it came from Grace. "I appreciate that."

"Tell them what happened yesterday, Dot," Phillip said as he nudged his wife gently.

"It doesn't have any bearing on the case. I already told you that," she said.

"Tell them anyway," Phillip insisted. He was the only person I knew who could get my mother to do something she didn't want to do, with the possible exception of me.

Momma paused for a few moments, and then she spoke in soft tones. "I may have threatened him yesterday, and other people may have overheard it."

I knew they hadn't gotten along, but a threat coming just before a murder was *never* a good thing. "What exactly did you say to him, Momma, and who overheard it?"

"I told him that if he didn't drop those suits, I'd bury him," she admitted.

That sounded bad. "Who overheard you?"

"Gabby Williams," Momma answered.

"How did she react?" Grace asked.

"As a matter of fact, she applauded the sentiment," my mother admitted. "Gabby hasn't been a fan of Gary Shook's since he came to town."

"The number of people Gabby doesn't get along with is a very long list indeed," I said.

"True enough, but she likes you, Suzanne," Grace said.

"What can I say? I'm lovable."

"I said like, not love, but maybe what I should have said was that she tolerates you," Grace replied with the hint of a grin.

"That's more than you can say for most folks around here, so I'll take it," I said. "Momma, do you think Gabby told anyone what she overheard?" Maybe we could put a lid on the news of Momma's threat if I could get to Gabby Williams before she started blabbing it all over town.

"I'm afraid that particular cat is well out of its bag," Momma admitted. "Perhaps I was a bit harsh on Gary, but he was becoming a real thorn in my side, and I wanted him to stop his foolish behavior."

I looked around to see if anyone was listening to us at the moment. Fortunately, the crowds were mostly milling around the grill and the bookstore tables, but I still didn't want to take any chances on who might overhear our conversation. In a soft voice, I said, "Momma, maybe it would be a good idea *not* to keep saying things like that."

She frowned. "Suzanne Hart, I didn't do it!" So much for wishing that Momma would keep her voice down, or even adjust what she said in public. Honestly, I should have known better than to even expect it.

Momma had certainly gotten folks' attention now. There were several people watching us as surreptitiously as they could manage it, but I knew they were hanging on every word, so what I said next was going to be very important. "Okay, take it easy, Momma," I said in an equally loud voice. "Maybe *I'm* the one who left the front door unlocked yesterday," I nearly shouted. It was lame, and what was more, I knew it, but it was the best I could do given the urgency we were facing.

I glanced around and saw that most folks went back to their own business when they found out how mundane our conversation appeared to be, so maybe it had worked well enough after all.

Chapter 5

I CAUGHT GRACE'S GLANCE, and she grinned at me. "That was smooth, Suzanne, really smooth," she said softly.

"Hey, it worked, didn't it?" I asked her.

"Against all odds, maybe," Grace replied.

"Momma, do you have any idea who might have killed Gary Shook?" I asked her.

"Phillip and I have been discussing it ever since we heard the news," she admitted, sporting a worried brow. Apparently my mother wasn't as disinterested as she'd pretended to be. She'd taken part in helping me solve a few cases in the past, and she'd been really good at it. Was it possible that she'd gotten a taste for amateur sleuthing herself?

"Were you able to come up with any candidates?" I asked her.

"We did, but I can tell you up front that you won't like the first name on our list," she told me.

"Jenny didn't do it," I told her point-blank.

"Are you honestly *that* positive about her innocence?" Momma asked me softly. "Suzanne, I know how loyal you are to your friends and family, but sometimes the most obvious suspect is the correct one."

"I know that," I told her, "but Jenny didn't do it. Why would she? She was getting out from under Gary Shook's thumb once and for all. Today was the last time she was ever going to have to do business with the man, so she didn't have a motive to kill him."

"Did she even have the final payment she owed him?" Phillip asked. I knew he didn't want to upset me, but it was clearly something he wanted to know.

"Believe me, she made *more* than enough today to pay her rent and her suppliers," I told him. As I waved toward Paige and Trish, I explained, "Since we've already covered her bills, this is all going toward Jenny's fund to start a new life. Why would she take a chance on ruining that forever just when she could see the light at the end of the tunnel?"

"Maybe he backed her into a corner, literally," Phillip suggested. "I've heard that Gary could be a bit handsy with some of his tenants."

"Where did you hear that?" I asked him.

"Phillip, that's nothing more than a salacious rumor you heard a few days ago at the barbershop," Momma said. "Do you honestly give that idle speculation credence?"

"Dot, you know as well as I do that sometimes where there's smoke, there actually is fire," he answered.

"Which tenant in particular did he make a pass at?" Grace asked.

"Molly Davis," Phillip said. "Curt Menninger walked in on them in the sewing shop a few days ago."

"What was Curt doing in the sewing shop?" I asked. I knew the gruff older man, and he didn't look like someone who would be caught dead in a place like that. Molly was thin, sporting nearly no curves at all, and in general not a woman who men seemed to notice.

"He was picking up a kit for his granddaughter," Phillip said. "You wouldn't believe how that eight-year-old girl has him wrapped around her little finger."

"Let's get back to the story," Grace suggested.

"Curt told everyone there that when he walked into the shop, Gary had a hand imprint on his face and Molly looked as though she was ready to burst out into tears. He told us that Gary tore out of there like he was on fire, but before he left, he gave Molly a look that would have frozen lava."

"Curt also believes that he was abducted by aliens as a toddler," Momma told us. "You can't believe *anything* the man says."

"I'm not saying that it's true that he hitched a ride on a UFO as a kid, but this story at least bears looking into, doesn't it?" Phillip asked. "Go on. Tell them what *you* heard, Dot."

"It's just more idle speculation," my mother said sternly. "I won't be a party to gossip."

"Momma, we need to know. Don't think of it as gossiping. Consider the fact that you're potentially helping bring a killer to justice."

"When you put it that way, how can I refuse?" she asked me as she studied me carefully. "When did you get so manipulative, young lady?"

"I like to think of it as just being persuasive," I corrected her.

"Yes, I'm sure you do," Momma answered.

"Dot, tell them," Phillip nudged her.

"Very well," Momma finally said with a sigh. "I was at the bank, moving some money around, when I overheard Gary and one of the new loan officers in the next room having an argument about something. I couldn't really hear more than the volume of their discussion, but it was clear that Gary said something to the young woman, because her face suddenly went stark white. Gary said something else softly to her, and then he walked out with a smug look on his face. She looked absolutely shattered. Two minutes later, I saw her gather her things and rush out of the building. Something happened between the two of them, but I have no idea what it might have been."

"Who was the banker?" I asked her.

"Cynthia Logan," she said, "but it could have been nothing more than a disagreement about a loan or something of that nature."

"Then it should be easy enough to clear up," I said. "Do you two have anything else for us?"

"No, but isn't that enough?" Momma asked.

I heard Trish call out, "Last call, folks. When this batch is gone, we're through."

"Come on, Dot," Phillip urged his wife. "You promised me a hot dog and a hamburger."

"Do you honestly need both?" she asked him.

His sheepish grin said it all. "*Need*? No, probably not. But *want*? You betcha."

My mother couldn't keep the stern expression on her face one second longer. "Let's get you fed, then, before you pass out from hunger."

"That's all I'm saying," he answered with a grin as he raced to get in a line that was forming quickly.

"Do you believe that?" I asked Grace.

"I don't blame him for hurrying," she said. "These things are amazing," she added as she finished her own burger.

"I'm talking about Molly Davis and Cynthia Logan," I said. I knew Molly, and I'd met Cynthia a few times in my donut shop. Cynthia was a tall, shapely, good-natured woman who enjoyed cinnamon in every way, shape, and form, from donuts to laced coffee to who knew what else. What in the world had Gary said to ice her that way?

"Gary Shook clearly had a talent for rubbing people the wrong way. Why are you so surprised, given what happened to him?"

"I guess I shouldn't be," I said. "Molly kind of surprises me, though."

"I don't know. If Gary really did make a hard pass at her, I can easily see her lighting him up with a slap. Knowing Gary, it might have been the only way she could be sure of getting his attention. I'm guessing we're going to go talk to both women once we're through here, right?"

"I think we should," I said as I saw her glancing back over at Trish's line. "Are you honestly still hungry after what we just ate?"

"You heard Trish. Once these are gone, they're gone."

"Fine. How about if I split another hot dog with you?" I asked her.

"I have to *share*?" she asked, clearly unhappy about my proposal.

"Perish the thought. We'll *each* get one," I said as I followed her to the line. Phillip smiled, and Momma just shook her head as we walked past them to join the queue. "Can we order for you, too?" my stepfather asked as he looked at the back of the line. "It might be the only way you're going to get seconds."

"Thanks," I said as I noticed that someone else was getting in line, too. "On second thought, we don't mind waiting," I said as I headed to grab the spot while I could.

"We don't?" Grace asked.

I pointed to the back of the line, and that was when she spotted Molly, too. "Thanks anyway," she said as we rushed to grab the spot.

Phillip and Momma looked at us both oddly until they saw Molly as well. Clearly it all suddenly made sense to them as well.

It appeared that we were about to get the opportunity to interview one of our suspects and get more delightful food all at the same time.

"Hey, Molly, how are you doing?" I asked the forty-something, rail-thin woman who owned the only sewing shop in town. Actually, we were probably lucky to have even one. If it weren't for the classes she taught on the side, I didn't know how she made her nut every month.

"I'm so-so," she said with a smile.

Grace laughed. "Would you spell that S.E.W., S.E.W.?"

"I would," Molly replied with a gentle smile.

"Sew Fine is a great name for your shop," I told her. "I played around with some other names before I called my place Donut Hearts."

"With you being named Hart, how could you resist?" Molly asked. "I love to read cozy mysteries with wordplay in their titles."

"I enjoy those, too," I said. "How are you holding up, given what happened earlier today?"

Molly's smile vanished. "What happened?" Did she pause a fraction too long before she answered my question?

"I'm talking about Gary Shook," I said.

"What about him?" she asked, this time a little timelier with her query.

"He's dead, Molly," I told her.

"No, he's not," Molly replied without making eye contact with either one of us.

"We found the body, and he's at the morgue by now, so I hope it's true," Grace said bluntly.

That caught Molly's full attention. "What? When? What happened? How did he die?"

"Somebody stabbed him in the heart with a lawn flag holder," I said.

She crinkled one eyebrow in my direction. "Seriously?"

"Seriously," I replied. "Have you spoken with the police yet?"

My question clearly caught her by surprise. "The police? Why should they want to speak with me?"

"We heard about what happened at Sew Fine," Grace said. "Half the town knows too, unless I miss my guess."

"I can't believe this is happening to me," Molly replied, clearly more upset to learn that word had gotten out about her confrontation with the murder victim than about his actual demise.

"It's not so great for Gary, either," Grace said. Blunt but true.

"I'm sorry. I don't want to talk about it. I've got to go," she said as she cut out of the line and headed toward her shop.

"You can stay if you want, but I'm going," I told Grace as I took off after Molly.

To my friend's credit, she didn't even look back at Trish's portable grill as she joined me.

"Where are you going in such a hurry?" I asked Molly as we finally caught up to her.

"I need to tell Lawrence and Cheryl," she said.

"Lawrence Grimes and Cheryl Simmons?" Grace asked her.

"They are both other tenants of Gary's," she replied.

"I have a feeling the police will be speaking with them as well," I said. "What really happened between the two of you, Molly?"

"I don't want to talk about it," she said as we neared her shop. There was a sign on the front door that said "Back in Five." I was guessing she'd been gone less than that, but then again, she hadn't counted on running into us. As Molly unlocked the door, we tried to follow her in, but she blocked our way. "Sorry, but I need to be alone."

"We understand," I said.

Grace looked at me oddly as Molly locked the door behind her, barring us from her shop. "We do?"

"Grace, we can't *make* her talk to us," I said. "Besides, the way I see it, we've got two other suspects nearby. Let's go see what they have to say for themselves."

"Should we split up or interview them together?" she asked me.

"As tempting as it is to divide and conquer, I think we need to stick together," I told her. Momma's warning still echoed in my ears, and I had to wonder if Grace was thinking about her caveat as well.

"Together works for me," she said.

Grace put a hand on the door to the shop Lawrence Grimes ran. I'd never been in there before, but then again, I wasn't his target audience. Big Larry's featured clothing for large men, and I didn't mean tall, at least not specifically. Lawrence was a huge fan of my donuts, buying five dozen mixed treats every Monday morning since he'd opened his shop. I knew that he also bought pastries, cookies, brownies, and other goodies from places in the area to keep his customers happy *and* keep them heavy enough for his clothing.

The first thing we saw when we walked in was one of the biggest manikins I'd ever seen in my life sporting plaid green-and-yellow pants and a hot-pink shirt that should have come with sunglasses.

"How do you like Manny's outfit?" Lawrence asked us as he approached us.

"Manny, as in manikin?" I asked him.

Lawrence nodded. "He's a fixture around here. Would you ladies like some brownies? Betty Wilkers from Union Square made them fresh this morning." He offered a tray with the most decadent-looking treats I'd ever seen. The chocolate brownies themselves would have been quite a lot, but with the fudge icing and heavy sprinkles of shaved chocolate on top, they looked absolutely sinful. "Don't worry about the calories," Lawrence said with a smile. "They don't count if you eat them standing up."

"If that were true, I'd weigh a hundred pounds," I told him.

"Yeah, me too," he admitted. "I'm not sure why you two are here. The police chief and Jake are both so skinny it's painful for me to see them walking down the street." I wasn't sure what counted as being slim to Lawrence. He barely topped five and a half feet, but if he weighed an ounce less than three hundred pounds, I'd have to see the scale myself to believe it.

"We wanted to talk to you about Gary Shook," I said.

Lawrence's good-natured smile quickly faded. "Yeah, I heard someone stabbed him with some kind of spear."

"Actually, it was a decorative yard flagpole," I said.

"Well, you know how those things go. They always get bigger the more times the story gets told," Lawrence said as he idly reached down and grabbed a brownie. As he popped the entire thing into his mouth, I had to wonder if he loved it that much or if he was trying to stay in touch with his base core of customers.

"Did he raise your rent, too?" Grace asked him.

"He tried, but I told him I wouldn't stand for it," Lawrence said.

"How did he react to that?" I asked.

"Listen, I know he's dead and you're not supposed to speak ill and all that, but the man was a bully and a coward. In my life, I've learned that the only way to deal with a bully is to get in their face and bully them right back. You think I don't know how to handle myself with his type? I've been bullied all my life because of my weight, and I learned early on that the only way to handle them is to not be afraid to fight back."

"Do you mean that literally?" I asked him gently. There had been a genuine fire in his expression as he'd shared his personal history with us. If you'd have asked me before if Lawrence had been capable of skewering Gary Shook, I would have said that it was doubtful.

Now I wasn't quite so sure.

"Did I stick him with that metal post? No, not that I can prove it one way or the other, but I can certainly sympathize with whoever did do it," he said.

"What did he do when you stood up to him?" I asked him.

"He blustered and blew off some steam, but he knew that I was serious."

"What would you have done if he hadn't backed down with his demands?" Grace asked him.

Lawrence shrugged. "I can move this shop in a day if I have to, and there are other storefronts I could rent in April Springs if I decided to stay in town. Then again, I've had offers to buy my shop, and one of these days, I might just take someone up on it."

"Is business always this slow?" I asked as I looked around the empty store.

Lawrence sported a brief frown. "Not always, but there are too many people on a health kick these days, always trying to lose weight. Let me ask you something, Suzanne. We're kind of in the same business. At least we share a big chunk of the same clientele. Is it worth it living five years longer if you're miserable while you're doing it surviving on grass and weeds?"

"I know my donuts aren't health food," I said, tired of having the exact same discussion yet again. It seemed I spent half my life justifying offering donuts to the world instead of wheatgrass smoothies and no-fat/no-calories/no-taste goodies. "But I don't recommend a steady diet of them to anyone. We have to make our own decisions in this life."

"Exactly," he said as though I'd just proved his point, which I hadn't. "People are going to indulge, and when they do, they shouldn't have to feel guilty about it. My clothes allow them to go out and look good even if they aren't at their target weight. We're both offering public services to the community. And are we rewarded for it? We are not," he said and then caught himself. "Sorry, I didn't mean to rant at you two. It just gripes me that some folks look down on me for what I do for a living."

It might have had something to do with enabling his customer base with free treats everywhere, but I certainly wasn't going to cast the first stone. Were some of my customers overweight? Absolutely, but who was I to deny them a simple pleasure in their lives? I wasn't exactly a fashion model myself, but I was starting to embrace my size and not spend my life worrying about those extra fifteen pounds I always seemed to be carrying around. It might not have been exactly healthy, but I was willing to live with the risk if it made me happy.

"Getting back to Gary Shook," I said. "Where were you this morning?"

"I opened the shop at nine, just like always," he said, "and I've been here ever since."

"You didn't leave your shop at all? If we ask around town, will there be anybody who might contradict that claim?" Grace asked him.

He shrugged. "I stepped out into the back room for a quick bite of lunch at twelve, but that was it."

"Do you stay open?" I asked.

"No, I lock the doors for fifteen minutes every day. My customers know not to come by, or if they do, they wait. I can't afford to hire someone to work here with me, and a man's got to eat, doesn't he?" he asked with a grin.

"So does a woman," I agreed, "but you have fifteen minutes that are unaccounted for, and what's worse for you is that those fifteen minutes could have been when Gary Shook was murdered," I said somberly. We didn't have an exact time of death, but I knew that it was possible for Lawrence to have slipped out the back way, snuck into the nearby bird shop, killed Gary Shook, and still have been back before anyone noticed that he was gone. If he'd skipped lunch to kill his landlord, it could explain why he was snacking so heavily on brownies at the moment, too. Then again, given his bulk, perhaps that *was* his regular routine.

"Maybe so, but I didn't do it. I can show you the empty Tupperware container from my lunch, but I can't prove that I ate it today and not yesterday. I guess we're at an impasse as far as an alibi for me goes."

"Lawrence, who do you think might have wanted to kill him?" I asked him. It was clearly time to change tack.

The big man frowned a moment before answering, and I watched as he reached for another brownie. I wasn't entirely certain that he was even aware of what he was doing. He ate half the treat and then after a moment said, "I don't like to point fingers at my friends, you know?"

"Lawrence, what you tell us will stay between us unless it's vital that the police know," I told him.

"You can trust us to be discreet," Grace added.

"Okay, but I still don't like doing it. Have you spoken with Jenny?" he asked as he glanced toward the spot that so recently housed For The Birds. "She's the most obvious suspect, wouldn't you say?"

"Some folks might feel that way," I said, "but if she was the one who actually did it, I don't think she'd have asked us to look into what really happened for her, do you?"

"She did that, huh?" he asked. "Maybe I'm wrong. Then again, maybe it's a bit of misdirection on her part. What better way to prove her innocence to you than to ask you to investigate the case on her behalf? It's kind of cagey if you ask me."

"Is there anyone besides Jenny you suspect?" Grace asked him.

Lawrence frowned. "If it had happened at Molly Davis's shop, I would have had a different answer for you."

"Didn't she get along with Gary Shook?" I asked him.

"Nobody got along with Gary, at least as far as I know, but Molly was scared to death of the man. He had some kind of hold over her. It wasn't right. I tried to coax out of her why she was so jittery around him, but she wouldn't tell me a thing. You could ask Cheryl if you'd like. They're closer than we are."

"What about Cheryl?" I asked.

His pupils immediately dilated, and his face got a bit flushed. "Leave Cheryl out of this. She didn't do it."

"You sound really sure of that," I pushed.

"I'm telling you to look somewhere else."

There was no doubt he was threatening us, and I had to wonder why. It was time to change the subject. "If Molly was afraid of him, would she attack him, though?" I asked him.

"You'd be amazed by what someone might do when they're backed into a corner with no way out," Lawrence said sadly.

"It sounds as though you've had some experience with that yourself," I said sympathetically.

"I just hate to see *anyone* being bullied," he said.

"That really doesn't answer the question, though, does it?" Grace pressed.

He was spared from answering when a heavyset young man in ratty jeans walked in. "Excuse me sir, but do you have suits my size?" he asked, clearly uncomfortable coming in.

Lawrence acted as though the young man was his long-lost best friend. "Of course we do," he said as he offered him a brownie.

"I really shouldn't," the young man said as he studied the plate.

"I understand completely," Lawrence said as he put the tray down within both men's reaches. "Now, what's the occasion?"

"My big sister is getting married, and I'm giving her away," the young man said. "I want to look good for her," he said, his voice halting a bit as he said it.

"Trust me, she will be amazed by how dashing you are going to be," Lawrence said.

A spark of hope flitted across the young man's face, and I could see what Lawrence had been saying earlier. He was a refuge, and in his own way, he was performing more of a public service than my donuts could ever provide. I had new respect for the man as he turned to us and said, "If you ladies will excuse us, I have work to do."

"Of course," I said as Grace and I exited.

"He's really slick, isn't he?" Grace asked me once we were out in front of the shop.

"What do you mean?" I asked.

"All I'm saying is that the man could sell ice in Antarctica," she replied. "Suzanne, he got to you, didn't he?"

"Maybe a little," I answered. "Grace, *am* I enabling people who can't help themselves around treats?"

"Suzanne, you offer a much-needed point of brightness in a world that is all too often full of darkness and despair. You're not responsible for everyone who comes into your shop. As long as I've known you, I've *never* seen you force anything on anyone else they didn't want. Lawrence is the one giving out free samples to keep his customers in his database, not you."

"Maybe, but at least he's helping that young man, which is something I sometimes wonder if I ever do."

"You're being way too hard on yourself. Think about the kind of customers you get," she said, taking my hands in hers. "You get the kid who flunked her algebra test in school and needs something to make her smile again, if only for a moment, the heartbroken man who's lost the woman in his life and is looking for a reason not to just give up, the couple wanting to celebrate a special moment in their lives with one of your treats. There are a thousand different reasons people come to Donut Hearts, but I suspect quite a few of them visit just to see your smile."

It was a moment of honest emotion for Grace, and it was clearly heartfelt. "You're right. Sorry, I just got a little lost."

"That's why I'm here, to keep you on the straight and narrow," she said with a grin.

"Grace, if I need *you* to keep me on the straight and narrow, then we're both in trouble," I said with a slight hint of laughter.

"Maybe, but if we do stray off the path, at least we'll each have good company," she added with a broad smile. "Now come on, let's go talk to Cheryl Simmons and see what *her* relationship with Gary Shook was. After all, we can't just take Lawrence's word for it."

It was a good idea, but at least for the moment, it was not to be.

There was a sign on the front door of Cheryl's nail salon that simply said, "Closed Until Further Notice."

How long had that sign been on the door, and what exactly did it mean?

I was about to ask Grace how we might find out when I saw someone coming our way, and she looked spitting mad at first glance.

Evidently Molly's ire with us both had escalated beyond the high level it had been at earlier, and I couldn't help wondering what exactly she was so angry about.

I had a hunch that we were about to find out though.

Chapter 6

"SUZANNE, WHAT DO YOU and Grace think you're doing?" Molly asked us hotly.

"It's a free world, Molly," I said. "You're not the only one we want to talk to."

"What did Lawrence say?" she pressed.

"Mostly we were learning a lot about his business model," Grace answered.

"We all know that you weren't there getting tips on running a men's clothing shop," she said.

"We were asking him about Gary Shook's murder," I replied, tired of being pushed about trying to find a killer.

"What did he tell you? Let me guess. He told you that he didn't do it."

"As a matter of fact, he did," I said.

"And you believed him?" she asked.

"Why shouldn't we? Do you know something we don't?" Grace asked pointedly.

"I know Lawrence has a temper. I've seen it before, and it's not pretty."

Wow. The big guy had done his best *not* to implicate his fellow renters, but apparently Molly had no such compunction. "Do you think he killed Gary Shook?" I asked.

"No, of course I don't," Molly said. Evidently she regretted trying to taint him with her last statement and was now trying to walk it back. "Cheryl didn't do it, either."

"Where is she, by the way? We saw that her shop was closed until further notice."

Molly frowned. "Cheryl's been having just as many problems as Jenny's had lately, but no one was eager to throw *her* a fundraiser," she said with a hint of ire in her voice. "I guess she just doesn't know the right people."

"We had no idea she was in trouble," I said. Was that how it looked to the rest of April Springs, that we were playing favorites with failing businesses? There wasn't anything we could do about that. I had been friends with Jenny for years, but Cheryl and I had barely spoken half a dozen times in the past decade. We all have our own circles, and of course we'd go out of our way to help those closest to us. It wasn't that we wouldn't have done something similar for Cheryl if we'd known about it, but Jenny's problems had been much more apparent to us.

"Of course you didn't," Molly said. "The April Springs Cool Kids wouldn't be friends with someone who runs a nail salon."

I was about to say something in our defense when Grace spoke up. "That's not fair, and you know it, Molly. We get that you're upset, but there's no reason to be mean about it."

She started to say something, and then I could see her collapse a little. "You're right. I'm sorry. I'm so worried about what's been happening around here lately that I'm lashing out at everybody within reach."

I smiled softly. "Just for the record, no one's ever accused me of being a cool kid in my entire life, Molly."

"I can vouch for that," Grace added happily.

"Hey, there's no reason for you to pile on, too," I said.

"Sorry," my best friend answered with a grin, but I doubted that she was sorry at all.

"Molly, we understand you're upset, but we can help you," I told her.

"How could you possibly do that?"

"Talk to us," I said, coaxing her a little. "The more we know, the more we'll be in a position to keep you out of this mess, and that's what you want, isn't it?"

"More than just about anything else in the world," she said with a sigh. "Come into the shop, and we'll talk."

"Good," I said as I touched her shoulder lightly.

Grace reached out and tapped my arm. When I glanced at her, she pointed in the direction of Lawrence's shop. He was trying to be stealthy about it, but it was clear that he'd been watching us the entire time. What about his customer? Had he just abandoned him in an effort to see what we were up to? The young man we'd met must have called out to him from the dressing room, because Lawrence quickly turned away from the window and headed out of sight.

Either that or he realized that we'd seen him.

What was he so worried about, anyway? Was there more to his story than he'd shared with us earlier? Had he really taken his lunch when he'd claimed to, or had he snuck out of his shop for something much more sinister? We'd have to dig a little deeper into the man's life, but for now, it appeared that Molly was going to at least give us something we might be able to use in either clearing her or pursuing her harder as a legitimate murder suspect.

"First things first," Grace said the moment we were in the sewing shop's craft room. A fourth of the store had been devoted to broad tables, comfortable chairs, sewing machines, and tons and tons of supplies. "Do you have an alibi between eleven and one today?" Those times represented when Jenny had gone into that supply room alone and the hour we'd found the body, so unless she had been lying to us, Gary Shook had been murdered sometime within those two hours.

"No, I sure don't," Molly said quickly.

"No?" I asked. "You're not even going to *try* to protect yourself?"

"I can't do it," she admitted. "I closed the shop at ten when I realized that no one was going to come in, and I didn't reopen until two. You might have been doing Jenny a nice favor, but you literally killed any business the rest of us could have hoped for today."

I hadn't even considered that as a possibility. By doing something nice for a friend, we'd inadvertently made life harder on a handful of other small businesses struggling to get through the day as well. In the process, we'd probably angered half a dozen folks with our genuinely generous act of kindness as well. I guess sometimes it was true what they said; no good deed ever goes unpunished.

"I'm sorry about that," I said.

"You mean that, don't you?" Molly asked.

"Of course I mean it. I run a small business too, remember? I know from firsthand experience how hard it is to make expenses some weeks."

"Try some months," she corrected me.

"Is your business slow right now, too?" Grace asked her.

"I'm getting by, but that doesn't mean that I'm not dipping into my savings some to bridge the gaps, too," she admitted. "That's why Gary's rent increase hit so hard. We're all already feeling the pinch of things slowing down, so this came as a double shock to our bottom lines and our financial plans." Molly laughed with more than a hint of irony in it. "That makes it sound as though I know what I'm doing, saying that I have a financial plan. The truth of the matter is that I'm just trying to stay afloat one more month in the hope that things will turn around soon before I have to shut down, too."

"It's tough, isn't it?" I asked her.

"At least you can eat your products that don't sell," Molly said with a shrug.

"That's true," I answered. "So, you weren't happy with Gary Shook either, would that be fair to say? Did you two argue a lot?"

"I wasn't pleased about the rent increase, and we had our share of confrontations, but that doesn't mean that I wanted to kill him," she answered.

"What about the other thing?" Grace asked her gently. "Molly, what *really* happened between you and Gary Shook the day someone walked in on the two of you?"

"Curt Menninger has a big mouth," Molly said in disgust.

"He wasn't lying though, was he?" I asked her.

"No, he wasn't," she admitted. "When I told Gary that I wasn't going to be able to make the new rent, he suggested that there were other ways I might be able to cover my monthly obligations, if you know what I mean."

I knew, and so did Grace. "Is that when you slapped him?"

"Wouldn't you?" she asked Grace.

"I would have done quite a bit more than just slap him," she said as she nodded in approval.

"Don't forget, Curt barged in on us before things got out of hand," Molly said with pursed lips.

"So then you would have gone further if you hadn't been interrupted at that moment?" I asked her.

Molly shrugged. "Who knows? I might have, but it doesn't matter. Curt did walk in, and Gary stormed off. That was the end of it as far as I was concerned."

"How about Gary? Was there any chance he was just going to let it go?" I asked.

"I can't say what that man would or would not have done, and there's no way to ask him that now, so what does it matter? I'm doing my best to forget that it ever happened."

"I'm not sure that's going to be possible," I told her.

"Why wouldn't it be?" she asked me. "Have you told anyone what Curt said?"

"No, but we aren't the only ones who know," I said. "Molly, the police are going to want to hear what happened, and unless I miss my guess, it's going to be sooner rather than later."

Her face lost a great deal of its color the moment I said it. "Isn't there *anything* I can do to make them leave me alone?" she asked, her voice almost a whine.

"You can tell them the truth, and I mean about everything," I said. "That's your only way out of this mess." I wanted to add, *If you didn't actually kill him*, but I decided to keep that particular statement to myself.

"It's going to look bad though, isn't it?" she asked.

"Maybe, but lying about what happened is just going to make it worse," Grace said.

"That's easy for you to say," she told Grace.

"Why do you say that?"

"The chief of police is your fiancé, isn't he?" Molly's question was almost an accusation.

"If I was the one in your shoes, I'd do the exact same thing that Suzanne and I are recommending you do," she said. "Fiancé or not."

I saw someone approaching the shop through the glass window of the craft room and reached out to touch Molly's hand. "It looks as though you're going to get the chance sooner than you think to do the right thing."

"Why do you say that?"

"Because the police chief is about to come into Sew Fine," I told her.

Chief Grant looked a bit surprised when he saw that Grace and I were already there, and as we all walked out together to join him, he said, "Fancy running into you ladies here."

"We were just paving the way for you," Grace told him with a slight smile.

"I appreciate that," he replied with a hint of a smile before it vanished quickly. "Do you have a second, Molly? We need to talk."

"At the police station?" she asked him, the fear thick in her voice.

"I don't see any reason it has to come to that," the chief said amiably. "Why don't we go back in there where we have some privacy?" He glanced at Grace and me to be sure we got the hint, but I didn't believe he thought for one second that we could have possibly missed it.

"We'll leave you both to it then," Grace said. "Come on, Suzanne."

I started to follow her, but before I did, I stopped and reached out to squeeze Molly's hand. "You're going to be okay, do you hear me?"

She looked pleased to get the small amount of comfort I could offer her. "Thanks. I appreciate that. I didn't mean what I said before, okay?"

"No worries," I told her with a reassuring smile. Chief Grant looked at me oddly, but I just shrugged in response. "Come on, Grace."

"I'm just waiting for you," she said with a grin.

I hated leaving Molly alone for her interview with the police chief, but there was really no way I could force myself to be a part of that particular conversation. Besides, if she hadn't been the one who'd killed Gary Shook, she had nothing to worry about.

It was an awfully big if, though.

Just because I had sympathy for her in this particular situation didn't mean that I'd given her a free pass, or Lawrence Grimes one either, for that matter. Neither one of them had done a thing to convince me of their innocence, and until I was sure of that, they were both going to stay on our list of suspects. Besides Jenny, that just left Cheryl Simmons to interview, and at the moment, we had no idea where she was or even how to find her.

Chapter 7

"SO, HOW DO WE FIND Cheryl?" Grace asked me as we headed back toward Donut Hearts. We'd been gone much longer than I'd anticipated, but that was how our investigations went sometimes. You followed one lead to the next and hopefully to the next without running into a dead end.

"We can go by her home," I said.

"I hope you know where she lives then, because I surely don't," she admitted.

"No, but I'm sure *someone* in town will know. I'm pretty confident in our resources, aren't you?" I asked her.

"You more than me. *Everyone* knows the donut lady," she replied with a grin.

"That's not entirely true, but I do get around," I admitted.

"On to more important matters," Grace said. "Do you think there's a mouse's whisker of a chance that Trish is still selling food?"

I glanced over at my friend. "Probably not, but even if she was, are you honestly still hungry? I figured a hot dog and a hamburger apiece would fill us up."

"It did, but that was quite a walk we just went on," Grace said with a frown.

"Maybe two miles round trip," I said.

"Hey, whose side are you on, anyway?" Grace asked me.

"Yours. Always yours," I said, and then I added, "I could probably use a bite myself."

"That a girl," she approved with a nod.

When we got back to the park where Trish had been parked before though, there was bad news for us.

The grill was chugging across the Boxcar Grill's parking lot behind the mayor's shiny new tractor.

It was clear that we wouldn't be getting any more food, at least not for the moment.

"I've got good news and bad news," Phillip said as we approached him as he finished his hot dog. The hamburger was nowhere in sight, so I had to assume that it was gone as well. "Which would you like first?"

"I'll take the bad news," I said. "I'd rather get that part out of the way so I can at least enjoy a bit of the good news."

He appeared to think about it a moment before saying, "No, I think I'll give you the good news first."

I looked over to see Momma heading in our direction, and she didn't look all that happy about something.

"Okay, shoot," I said.

"I ordered an extra hamburger and hot dog for you," Phillip said.

"And the bad news?" I asked, though I suspected I already knew what it was.

"I wasn't sure you were coming back. You were gone so long," he said, clearly remorseful.

"So you ate them both for us," I finished the thought. "Please tell me that's the bad news and not something more calamitous than that."

"It's going to be bad enough when your mother finds out what I did," Phillip said ruefully. "Is there any chance you'd cover for me?"

I laughed, and Grace followed suit. "Not a chance, Buster. You're on your own." I patted his shoulder as I added, "It's time to put on your big-boy pants and fess up, Phillip."

"What is so amusing?" Momma asked as she approached us.

"Phillip has something to tell you," I said to her. "Don't mind us. We were just leaving."

"Stay," Momma ordered both of us.

The last thing I wanted was to be within a hundred yards of the two of them when Phillip broke the news of his eating binge to my mother, but there was something about that commanding voice of hers that

I just couldn't bring myself to defy, and from the expression on Grace's face, she couldn't do it either.

"Fine, but we had nothing to do with it," I said.

Phillip shot me a hangdog look before he turned to Momma. After taking a deep breath, he let the words spill out quickly, no doubt in order to get his confession over with. "I ordered an extra hamburger and hot dog for Suzanne and Grace, but when they didn't show up, I ate them myself."

We all braced for the backlash of this admission, but Momma barely cracked a frown. "You're a grown man, Phillip. If you want to indulge yourself every now and then, it's certainly none of my business."

My stepfather looked as shocked by the statement as I was. "Hang on a second, Momma," I said. "That's an awfully cavalier attitude to be taking, isn't it?"

"Suzanne, don't badger your mother," Phillip said quickly.

"I really want to know. Is this a new you, or is it just a one-time aberration?"

"Suzanne, I have more on my mind than my husband's eating habits at the moment. I've just been summoned to the police chief's office."

"Wow, that was fast," I said.

"How could he even be finished with Molly already?" Grace asked.

"Molly Davis? What did he want with her?" Momma asked, and then she quickly answered her own question. "She was one of Shook's renters, wasn't she? Does she have a motive, other than having to deal with that man on a regular basis?"

"Don't you mean *other* than the story I heard from Curt?" Phillip asked.

"Yes, of course," Momma said. "Surely the police chief didn't take that seriously."

"Dot, he's investigating a murder. What choice does he have? He has to follow every lead he gets. It's what I would do."

"Including bringing me in for questioning?" Momma asked fiercely.

"Yes, even that," he admitted. Good for him for sticking to his guns. There were only a few folks in seven counties that would be willing to do that with my mother. "You have to see things from his point of view."

"Right now, I don't have to be empathetic toward anyone but myself," Momma said. "I'm supposed to meet him in half an hour. Do I need an attorney?"

"If you want one, you should take one," I said. "I have a few names if you need them."

"Thank you, but I have resources of my own," she answered. "Phillip, what do you think? Would it make me look guilty if I had representation present?"

"Not necessarily," my stepfather hedged.

Momma took that in before speaking to him again. "Would you?"

"No," he said flatly. "I'd love to go with you, though. If things get out of hand, we can always shut it down and call someone, but I feel as though the right way to handle this is to go in with the intention of helping the police chief, not stonewalling him. Then again, I meant what I said. It's your call."

"I can see the sense in your advice. Would you mind if I got a second opinion?"

Phillip smiled. "Never, my love. As a matter of fact, it would get me off the hook, so I'm all for it. Ask anyone whose opinion you respect. I promise not to take offense."

"Thank you," she said before turning to me. "Suzanne? What are your thoughts on the matter?"

It took me a second to realize that she really wanted my opinion. Wow, did that ever feel good! I didn't hesitate. "I agree with Phillip. Go in with an open mind, but if the chief starts asking things you aren't comfortable with answering, shut it down."

Grace had been mostly silent up until that point, but she spoke up now. "Stephen's not going to try to railroad you, Dot. I promise you that."

Momma reached out and patted Grace's hand. "I didn't think he was, but I appreciate the fact that you feel compelled to stand up for him."

"Only when I'm sure he's doing the right thing," Grace said firmly. "I've got your back, too. Don't ever forget that."

"I couldn't even if I tried," Momma said as she took Grace's hand with one of hers and mine with the other one. "I don't tell you both enough, but I'm so proud of the women you've become."

That was the perfect opportunity for me to open my trap and blow it, but for once in my life, I stayed silent. I did give her a quick smile, one she returned in kind.

Grace was about to say something when her cell phone rang. After checking the caller ID, she said, "Sorry, I have to take this. It's my boss."

As she stepped away, I hoped she wasn't getting in trouble for giving away products and financing Jenny's going-out-of-business sale. Grace loved her job, and I prayed that her generosity hadn't put her in an awkward position with her supervisor. After nearly a minute, she hung up and rejoined us.

"Bad news?" I asked her with concern.

"On the contrary," Grace said with a look of wonder on her face. "She loved that I took the initiative today. As a matter of fact, she's putting me up for our monthly outstanding sales award. I've never even been nominated before."

"Do you get a fancy trophy or something if you win?" I teased, happy that Grace's actions had rewarded her as well, no matter how inadvertently.

"It's better than that. The winner gets a nice fat check and an extra week's vacation. Shoot, I'll take any of the runner-up prizes. The checks aren't nearly as fat and the vacation is only for a day, but it beats not even being nominated."

"I'll be pulling for you," I said.

"As will we all," Momma echoed. She glanced at her watch. "Phillip, let's go over there early. I want to get this over with."

"He's probably not back from speaking with Molly yet, Momma," I told her.

"Be that as it may, the waiting is adding too much stress I don't need in my life," she answered. "Coming, Phillip?" Momma added as she headed toward the police station, which honestly wasn't all that far away from where we were currently standing. That was one of the benefits of small-town living; just about everything was in walking distance.

"I'm right behind you," he said, and then he added softly to me, "I'll let you know what happens."

"Thanks. I appreciate that. Look out for her, okay?"

"I don't need the reminder, Suzanne. Your mother is my first priority in the world, and I don't care who knows it."

As he trotted off after her, I smiled. I hadn't always been a big fan of the man, but he was pretty high up in my book these days. I knew my mother was in good hands, so I'd try not to worry about her. I wasn't sure how successful I'd be, but at least I'd make the effort.

"So, should we go off looking for Cheryl now?" Grace asked me.

I looked around at the mess the park had become as well as the street in front of Donut Hearts. "I feel responsible for all of this," I said. "You can do what you want, but I'm going to stick around and help clean up first."

"I'm with you, rain or shine, trash or treasure," she said as her phone rang again. "Seriously? I just spoke with her. Is it possible that she's changed her mind already about nominating me?" As Grace took the call, I headed over to Donut Hearts, which had long been closed for the day under Emma and Sharon's expert supervision. Ducking into my storage space, I grabbed a box of trash bags and some disposable gloves.

I wasn't exactly sure what kind of garbage we'd be picking up, but it wouldn't hurt to be prepared.

When I came back out of Donut Hearts, Grace was standing there on the sidewalk waiting for me.

"You're not going to believe this," she said.

"What happened? Did she really change her mind that quickly?" What kind of boss did Grace work for if she could be that mercurial with her decisions?

"No, but in order to be nominated, I need to write up what we did today so she'll have something to submit to the committee. I'm so sorry, but I can't help you clean up right now."

"It's okay," I said. "Go! This is important."

"I swear I didn't plan it this way," she said with a shrug.

"I believe you," I said. I'd thought about teasing her about being saved by the bell, but I quickly decided that wouldn't be very nice. "Now go write that report. Do you need help with it?"

"You're kidding, right? Suzanne, I was *born* to embellish. This is going to be a piece of cake. I'm almost worried that it's going to be *too* convincing. After all, I'm happy where I am, so I don't want them deciding to make me a regional vice president or something."

"We both know that you're good, but are you really *that* good?" I asked her.

"The truth is that I'm even better than that," she answered with a grin as she headed down Springs Drive toward her house. I had to laugh when she started skipping home, and I was still smiling when I donned a pair of gloves, shook a trash bag open, and started collecting everyone else's discards.

But it was going to be a long afternoon if I was going to have to do it all by myself.

"Need a hand?" Jillian Moore asked me ten minutes into the job. I wouldn't have thought she'd volunteer to do anything as mundane as picking up garbage, but sometimes people surprised me in a good way, which was always a nice change of pace.

"The more the merrier," I said as I handed her a bag and an extra set of gloves.

"That's cute," Jillian said as she took them from me.

"What? The gloves?"

"No, using my last name. The Moore the merrier, right?" she asked, emphasizing her name.

It hadn't even occurred to me, but if she wanted to think I was clever, I wasn't about to dissuade her of the notion.

"Why not?" I asked.

I expected her to branch off and clean another area of the park, but she stayed close to me and continued to chat. "I had different plans this afternoon, but they were suddenly canceled on me."

"Because of the sale?" I asked her, wondering just how far-reaching the ramifications of our good deed had been.

"Who knows? It's not like Cheryl to just abandon me out of the blue like that." She held out a gloved hand and added, "If you could see my nails, you'd know just how desperate I am to have them done."

"You go to The Last Nail?" I asked.

"I have for years. It's a shame, really."

"That she canceled on you?" I asked.

"No, that she's probably going to have to throw in the towel. Her shop isn't doing all that well, and she's had an offer to work closer to home that she's probably going to have to take."

"Where might that be?"

"She lives in Union Square," Jillian said. "I'm not sure why she felt the need to open up a nail salon half an hour from home, but she did. Maybe she got a good deal on her rent, at first anyway."

"Why do you say that?"

Jillian looked around and saw that no one was paying any particular attention to us. "That landlord of hers was doubling her rent! She was barely getting by as it was, and then that? It was crazy. I told her that I'd follow her wherever she went, and most of my friends would too, but she hated the idea of having to give up on her dream. She's going through a nasty divorce from a very bad man. The poor girl just can't seem to get a break."

"Did she ask Gary Shook for a rent reduction?" I pondered aloud as I picked up a discarded plate smeared with catsup and mustard. Honestly, why would someone just throw it on the ground when there was a trash can not ten feet away? Littering was a pet peeve of mine. I liked things neat and orderly, especially in the park. After all, in a very real way, it was *all* part of my front yard.

"From Shook? Good luck with that. I had a feeling he might have done it if she'd given in to his advances, but she wasn't having any of that nonsense."

"Did she actually tell you that?" I asked, wondering why someone would share something like that with a client of all people.

"She didn't have to. I saw the man try to back her into a corner two weeks ago. I thought she was going to stab him with a metal nail file for a second there." Jillian frowned suddenly. "I shouldn't have said that. Forget you heard it from me."

"It's a tough thing to forget," I said. "You know Gary Shook was skewered with a metal shaft, don't you?"

"Cheryl didn't do it," Jillian insisted. "She's too sweet to commit murder."

"You'd be surprised," I said. "Where do you think she might be today?"

Jillian shrugged as she picked up a crumpled paper cup and put it into her bag. "I have no idea, Suzanne."

"But you have to admit that it's suspicious that she'd just vanish into thin air on the day her problematic landlord is murdered, don't you?"

"When did you suddenly go to law school?" Jillian asked me as she took a few steps away from me. "You're acting like a lawyer, or maybe even a cop. You're still just a donutmaker, right?"

"That's me, *just* a donutmaker," I said with a bitter smile and more than a little sarcasm in my voice. I'd been called that plenty of times before in my life, but it still irked me. It was insulting to call anyone *just* an anything. It assumed that was all that I was capable of. If Jillian had any idea how many murderers I'd had a hand in bringing to justice, she might have been a little more respectful.

"I didn't mean it that way," she said haltingly as she quickly backpedaled. "Look, Connie Hanks is over by the gazebo. I need to talk to her about something." Jillian headed off before I could stop her. Great, I'd antagonized someone who was actually helping my investigation all because she'd hurt my feelings a bit. It wasn't a very professional way to act, but then again I was an amateur, and proud of it. Just because no one paid me to solve crimes didn't mean that I wasn't good at it. Still, I shouldn't have been so transparent in my displeasure.

At least I'd learned a few valuable things about one of my suspects. Cheryl Simmons had some problems with the murder victim, and they weren't insubstantial ones, either. Grace and I had a place to start hunting for her, too. We weren't without resources in Union Square, and I wouldn't mind paying my friends at Napoli's a visit in a few hours. We'd be able to ask Angelica and her daughters about Cheryl and maybe get something to eat while we were there as well. It was a win-win situation in my book any day of the week, and with Jake out of town again, I had no dinner plans. Since the chief was working on a brand-new murder case, it would be nice to have Grace as a dinner companion, so why not mix a little food in with our investigation? It had certainly worked for us in the past.

Chapter 8

WE'D BEEN WORKING FOR close to an hour when we finally finished cleaning up. I had personally filled three bags and I'd started on another, and my opinion of some of my fellow residents of April Springs had plummeted since the project had begun. I decided that I was going to have to let that go though, or it would spoil the rest of my day, and I had too much still to do. As I surveyed the area, it looked nearly pristine to me again, something that I took a great deal of pride in helping achieve. Looked at from that perspective, it almost made me happy that we'd started with such a filthy scene just to get it looking so good again. To my surprise, more than a few folks had pitched in as well, so it had ended up being a team effort in the end.

Almost was the key word there, though.

The trash cans in the park were full, so I toted the first batch of bags toward my donut shop. I'd stash them back there with my other trash and let the city crew worry about them since our pickup day was tomorrow.

As I got closer, I noticed someone lurking behind Donut Hearts!

I was standing in bright sunshine and the side of the building was in shadow, so I couldn't really make much out but a moving person.

"Hey, hang on," I said as I dropped the trash bags and took off full speed toward my building.

Whoever had been there must have seen me coming, and they had ducked down the alley behind the shop instantly.

By the time I got back there, whoever it had been was long gone.

As I looked around for some trace of who had been there, Grace came up behind me.

"What just happened, Suzanne? I was walking over to you, and the next thing I knew, you were taking off like a rocket."

"Someone was back here lurking," I told her as I continued to scan the area. Whoever it was had left no trace of their presence, at least as far as I could see.

"*Lurking*?" Grace asked with a careful hint of a grin. "How exactly does someone *lurk*?"

"You know, stick to the shadows and run away when they're discovered," I explained. "You've lurked plenty of times yourself, so don't try to pretend you don't know what I'm talking about." I was on edge, so I must have been a little snippier than I'd meant to be.

"Hey, take it easy. I'm on your side, remember?"

I touched her arm lightly and smiled. "Sorry. It's just a little unnerving, you know?"

"I do," she said, "especially given Gary Shook's murder."

"Did you finish your report?" I asked her.

"Wrote it, polished it, proofed it, and sent it in," she said. "How did the cleanup go?"

"I learned some interesting things about Cheryl Simmons," I admitted.

"Suzanne, have you been sleuthing without me?" she asked, half teasing and half accusing me of improper behavior.

"It wasn't anything I did. The clues came to me," I said.

After I recounted everything Jillian Moore had told me, Grace nodded. "I'm guessing we're heading over to Union Square then, aren't we?"

"I'd like to, but first I'd like to see how Momma made out with Chief Grant."

"I wouldn't mind knowing that myself," Grace said firmly.

"Then let's walk over to the police station, shall we?" I asked.

"What about those trash bags?" she asked me.

I looked over and saw that the volunteer crew were getting them for me. "It appears that it's being taken care of even as we speak."

"Jillian's still helping, so you must not have offended her too badly," Grace said.

"I still shouldn't have been so abrupt with her," I admitted.

"Hey, you're human. You're entitled to get a little snippy sometimes."

"Even with you?" I asked her.

"Well, let's not get *too* carried away," she answered with a laugh.

"I'll do better, and that's a promise."

"Your best is plenty good enough for me," Grace said as we made our way to the nearby station. I wasn't sure how long we were going to have to wait on Momma and Phillip, but I was willing to stay there all afternoon and into the evening if that was what it took.

In the end, it didn't turn out to be any wait at all, though.

We ran into Momma and Phillip walking out of the station just as we were about to walk in, and from the look of things, my mother was not very happy with how things had turned out.

"Was it honestly *that* bad?" I asked her as we all regrouped out on the sidewalk in front of the station.

"It was dreadful," Momma said as Phillip answered, "Not so much."

"Which was it?" I asked them.

Momma spoke first. "It may not have been that bad for your stepfather, but then no one was accusing him of committing murder."

"Dot, he was just doing his job. He had to ask questions that needed to be answered."

"He asked me for an alibi!" Momma snapped at him.

I couldn't just let Phillip twist in the wind like that all by himself. "Momma, he's just trying to eliminate you as a suspect. What did you tell him?"

My mother turned on me with a glare that could melt plastic. "Suzanne Hart, do *you* suspect your own mother of murder?"

"No, of course not!" I said quickly, and as loudly as I could manage to boot. "I was just hoping that if you had an alibi, he'd take you off his list of potential suspects."

Grace spoke up. "Dot, we never even considered you a possibility, and that's the truth."

"Of course we didn't," I echoed.

"See?" Phillip asked my mother. "I *told* you that no one would think that you could have done it."

"I *could* have done it," my mother corrected him, "but I *didn't*."

"Is it really important that we make that distinction while we're standing in front of the police station?" I asked as a pair of cops I knew walked in, slowing only to bob their heads in my direction on their way into work. It had nothing to do with the fact they both loved my treats. Well, maybe it had a little to do with that, but they knew me as a person too and not just the lady who made donuts for them.

At least I thought they did.

"Were you able to give Stephen *anything*?" Grace asked her gently.

"What could I tell him but the truth? I was in a meeting," Momma admitted.

"But not the entire time," Phillip added.

"I could account for all but ten minutes of the time frame the police were asking about," Momma said sternly.

I didn't have the heart to tell her that ten minutes would have been more than enough to commit the murder and slip away unnoticed. Evidently Grace had no such compunction. "Dot, he's just doing his job. Stephen has to look at everyone, not just the folks he doesn't like."

"I know that, dear," Momma said. "But I don't have to enjoy the unwanted attention."

"Of course you don't," Grace said quickly. "Where did you leave things?"

"She's off his list for now, even with that ten-minute gap," Phillip said. "The ten minutes in question are at the beginning of the time frame, and even the chief admitted that it would be unlikely for Dot to have killed Gary Shook and then just gone about her business acting as though nothing had happened."

"That's ridiculous," Momma said. "He's not giving me nearly enough credit. I could have *easily* disguised the fact that I'd just killed someone from anyone."

"Not from me you couldn't," Phillip said.

"Me, either," I echoed.

Grace appeared to study my mother carefully before commenting. "I don't know. Dot, you're a pretty cool customer. Personally, I think you'd be able to do it."

"Thank you, my dear," Momma said, pleased for some reason that was beyond me. "Enough of this lunacy," she added, no doubt trying to move on from our current conversation. "Let's all have dinner tonight and put this madness behind us."

I thought about our plans to eat at Napoli's, but Momma's cooking was great too. Then again, I could have that whenever I wanted it without driving half an hour both ways, and since we were going to be in Union Square anyway, why not kill two birds with one stone?

"Suzanne, you're taking an *awfully* long time to answer," Momma said as she studied me carefully.

"We really appreciate the offer, but Grace and I are following up on a lead in Union Square, and we have no idea when we'll be back. Could we have a rain check?"

My mother nodded. "Enjoy Napoli's, and say hello to Angelica and her lovely daughters for me," she said.

"Me too," Phillip added hastily.

Momma glanced over at him, started to say something, and then just laughed instead. "You are forgiven for being a little too enthusiastic about that addendum," she told her husband.

He was smart enough not to even protest. "I appreciate that. Are you ready to head home?"

"I've been ready for what feels like days," my mother said.

As the two of them walked toward their vehicle, Phillip asked her, "I still get dinner though, right?"

She smiled as she took her husband's hand. "Have I ever *not* fed you, love?"

"No, and I'd hate for it to start now," he replied.

As we drove to Union Square, Grace asked, "Should we eat...I mean go to Napoli's first to find out what they might know about Cheryl, or should we just try to figure it out on our own?"

"I'm honestly not ready to eat dinner yet, are you?" I asked her.

"When it comes to Napoli's, I can *always* eat," Grace said with a smile.

"Yeah, I could, too," I admitted. "Tell you what. Let's go by the place where Cheryl used to work and see if they might know how we can find her."

"And if they don't know?" Grace asked.

"Then it's off to Napoli's we go," I agreed.

"That's all I'm asking," she said. "What do you think about what we know so far?"

"About the case, you mean? Please tell me that we're still not talking about food."

"Of course about the case," Grace said curtly. "Actually, I was thinking we could take the Trip for Two Around Italy at Napoli's. Are you game?"

I'd had that special before with Jake, and we'd taken food home afterwards. The portions were huge and plentiful. "Are you really up for that?"

"I'm not afraid to take home leftovers," Grace answered, "and I've never known you to shy away from them, either."

"That's a fair point," I said. "Okay, now that we've got the important stuff out of the way, let's talk about Gary Shook."

"He really was a bit of a weasel, wasn't he?" Grace asked me.

"Apparently more than I even realized," I admitted. "It's one thing to jack up the rent to the point where your tenants can't afford to stay there anymore, but using his position of power as a means to get at least one of those women to consider doing something they'd never dream of doing if they weren't under duress is a whole new level of low in my book."

"I *hate* people who take advantage of other people like that," she said. "It's the lowest form of life to me."

"I can think of some lower ones," I countered. "Like murderers, for instance."

Grace took a moment to compose herself before answering. "I'm not saying that Gary Shook deserved to be skewered like he was, but I can certainly understand the killer's motivation. Still, I agree with you. It's wrong."

"At least we're on the same page there, then," I said. "Anyway, we're doing this for Jenny, remember?"

"She's certainly had more than her share of grief in her life, hasn't she?"

"She has, but at least she found Margaret, so that's something," I added.

"They're both still suspects though, right?" Grace asked. "I mean despite the fact that Jenny asked us to find the killer. I still think it could be a smoke screen to keep us from thinking it was her."

"It would be a bold move though, wouldn't it?" I asked.

"Yes, but I think that's what *I* would do if I killed Gary Shook and you started digging into the murder, or if I even thought that there would be a possibility that you would discover that I was the one who'd done it," she answered.

"You give me too much credit," I said with a shrug. "I'm not that good."

"I don't agree with that statement at all, but even you have to admit that you've garnered quite a reputation around town as an amateur sleuth over the years."

"You have one too, don't forget," I reminded her.

"Maybe, but I've never solved a case without you, while you've solved a handful without me. That makes *you* the threat, not me," she said.

"Do folks around here really think of me as a *threat*?" I asked her as I slowed down without meaning to. If that were true, I wasn't all that pleased with my reputation. After all, who wanted to be thought of as a threat by the people she lived among? Had I pushed myself beyond the limits of what an average citizen should do when it came to investigating murder? I hadn't planned on it as a side career, but it had surely found me. That didn't mean that I had to keep doing it forever, though. Maybe it was time after this case to walk away from sleuthing once and for all. I knew that Jake and Momma would be more than a little bit relieved if I chose to hang it up. After all, I'd put myself in more situations that were dangerous than I ever would have thought possible for a simple donutmaker.

"Don't look so upset," Grace said, clearly trying to comfort me. "Maybe the bad guys think so, but the rest of us are grateful that you've been willing to step up and put your life on the line trying to keep us all safe."

"You make me sound more important than I really am," I protested.

"That's because you are more of a factor than you're ever willing to acknowledge," she replied. "Now let's get back to the case before we get to Union Square. No matter how much we might like them, we have to keep Jenny and Margaret on our list, Jenny because of her relationship with Gary Shook and Margaret because of her overwhelming desire to protect her birth daughter."

"That's fine, but my mother is *not* going on our list," I said bluntly.

"Suzanne, I would never dream of putting her there, and you know it," Grace said, sounding a bit offended by the mere suggestion.

I reached over and patted her knee. "I know that. Let's see, Molly has to be on it for a couple of reasons, and so do Cheryl and Lawrence. The truth is that *all* of Gary's renters had a reason to lash out at him, and this was a spur-of-the-moment murder if ever there was one."

"Why do you say that?"

"They slipped into the back of For The Birds, and the only way the killer would know to do that was if they followed him there. The murder weapon was a flagpole stored in the back room, and I doubt someone followed Gary Shook around with one waiting for the opportunity to stab him with it. That all makes it spontaneous to me."

"That's a fair point. How did they even know that someone like Jenny wouldn't walk in on them during the murder?" she asked.

"I don't think the killer even gave it a thought. Gary set someone off, they grabbed the closest weapon they could find, and then they stabbed him in the chest with the flag holder," I summed up, imagining the act in my mind. Unfortunately, I couldn't see the face of the killer, or our job would have been a great deal easier than it was.

"Is there anyone else we should consider?" Grace asked as we passed the Welcome to Union Square sign. "We're almost here."

"Did Gary have *any* kind of life outside of work?" I asked as I hunted for the town's only nail salon. It was named Nailed It The First Time, and there was a woman coming out I knew as I parked in front of the salon.

It was Cheryl Simmons.

The pudgy thirty-something woman was hard to miss with her outlandish outfit and her customary heavy makeup.

Talk about kismet. Finding her at least had turned out to be a great deal easier than I could have imagined.

Getting her to talk freely to us might be another matter entirely, but there was only one way to find out if that were true.

"Come on, Grace," I said as I turned off the Jeep.

She was a step behind me, so before Cheryl could escape, we hurried toward her to ask our questions.

Chapter 9

"HEY, CHERYL. WHAT are you doing, revisiting your old haunts?" I asked her as we approached.

The nail salon owner seemed startled to see us, especially given the fact that we weren't in April Springs. "Suzanne, Grace, what are you two doing here? Are you coming all the way over here to get your nails done?"

"As a matter of fact, we were looking for you," I admitted.

Cheryl looked shocked by the admission. "If you're hoping to get appointments at my salon, I'm afraid you're a bit too late."

"Why is that?" I asked her.

"I'm shutting it down. I just asked, begged is more like it, Naomi for my old job back, and she's agreed to take me back. I can't believe how much she made me grovel, though." The distaste for what she'd just done showed clearly on her face.

"What's going to happen to your business in April Springs?" Grace asked her.

"The truth is that it wasn't much of a business on my best day. I was barely scraping by, and then yesterday Gary Shook told me that he was jacking up my rent. I can see the writing on the wall. I'm shutting down, and I told him so. The worm didn't even try to stop me. Honestly, he acted as though he was *happy* I couldn't make the new rent. In fact, he told me that if I got out by the end of business Friday, he'd prorate my last month's rent. I didn't have much choice, so I agreed to do it."

"Why would he do that?" I asked. "Do you think he already has another tenant lined up to take your place?"

"That would be my guess," she said. "I don't know who could afford to pay that kind of rent increase, though. Molly and Lawrence surely wouldn't be able to do it."

Something nagged at the back of my mind, but I didn't have time to pursue it as Grace asked, "Did Gary Shook ever make a pass at you, Cheryl?"

She looked at Grace as though she'd slapped her. "Who told you about that?"

"It's true then?" I asked.

Cheryl frowned, and for a moment I thought she might start crying, but she finally managed to compose herself enough to talk to us. "It's true," she admitted. "That was another reason I didn't want to hang around any more than I had to. Listen, I'm not proud of myself, but I didn't have much choice, okay? I never actually did anything. I just gave him the impression that I might. Then, when he came by to collect yesterday, I came to my senses, and I threw him out. I'm almost out of a horrible relationship with a man I married out of desperation. I wasn't about to get involved with someone else so bad for me. I didn't sleep a wink all night worrying about what I should do, and this morning, I finally realized that I had to cut and run. I've been driving aimlessly around town for hours trying to get the nerve up to ask for my old job back, and I finally managed to do it. At least I'll get a little satisfaction telling Gary that I'm leaving."

Was it possible that she hadn't heard the news, or was she just acting? I couldn't tell, but then again, I wasn't exactly a human lie detector. There had been folks, even bad guys, who had lied to me before, and they probably would again if I decided to keep digging into murders that happened around me.

"He's dead, Cheryl," Grace said, and we both studied her.

"If wishing made it true, maybe, but I can't believe that it's true." She looked as though she thought we were teasing, but after a second or two, she must have realized that we weren't. "He's really dead? You're not kidding?"

"We're not," I said softly.

"What happened? Did he get hit by a bus or something? I can't believe this. Who do I give my notice to? Do you know who gets his rentals? This is a real mess."

One of her questions struck home. Who exactly *was* set to inherit Gary Shook's properties and the rest of his estate? That could certainly be a motive for murder. Greed often was, so we'd have to look into that.

"We don't have many answers at this point," I said. "Only questions."

It suddenly dawned on her why we were talking to her. "You didn't come here to get a nail appointment, did you? You two think I did it."

"You have to admit that you should be on the suspect list," Grace pushed.

"I'll admit no such thing! I didn't kill him, and I don't know who did!" She was practically shouting at us now. "As if I don't have enough to worry about right now." Cheryl stormed off, and Grace started after her.

I put a hand on my friend's shoulder. "Hold on."

"Aren't we going to at least *follow* her?" Grace asked as we watched the nail salon owner storm off in a huff.

"I have a feeling that she's given us everything we're going to get out of her at the moment," I said. "We have a motive for her, two actually, and she doesn't have much of an alibi, at least not one that we can confirm, unless we can find some people who saw her driving around. What else would you have asked her if she hadn't just stormed off?"

Grace nodded. "That's a good point. She protested a bit *too* loudly when she knew what we were suggesting, didn't she? Maybe a bit *too* much?"

"Maybe," I said. "Do you believe her?"

"About her weak alibi or her flat denial?" Grace asked me as we walked back to my Jeep.

"Both, as well as her claim that nothing happened between her and Gary yesterday," I said. "We only have her word about *any* of it, and

Gary Shook is not exactly in a position to dispute her version of what happened."

"So, you think she might have buckled under the pressure he was applying and then got remorseful and more than a little bit resentful after the fact?" Grace asked me.

"She could have been fuming about what happened and then she saw him duck into the back of For The Birds. Cheryl could have confronted him, and then when things escalated, she could have gotten revenge for what he'd forced her into doing against her will."

"Those are a lot of ifs," Grace said.

"Maybe so, but unless we can confirm that she was nowhere near April Springs all day, she's going to stay on our list."

"I agree with you," she said. "She brought up an interesting point though, didn't she?"

"About who inherits Gary Shook's estate? I was wondering about that, too."

"That wasn't what I was talking about, but that's certainly something we need to dig into, too."

"What were you referring to?" I asked her.

"Why was Gary in such a rush to get rid of all of his tenants? Who else could possibly afford to come into that strip mall and take over those businesses at those inflated rental prices?"

A thought suddenly struck me. "What if he didn't have any new tenants lined up at all?"

"That makes no sense at all to me," Grace answered.

"It does if he was selling the property outright, and in order to do so, he might have needed the businesses to be gone first," I said. "I need to call Momma."

"Can you do it on the way to Napoli's?" she asked. "It's getting close to dinnertime, and I want to be sure we get a table."

"Sure, I can talk and drive at the same time," I said as we got in and headed to our favorite place to eat in all of Union Square and beyond, though that was something I never would have admitted to Trish Granger, our friend who happened to own and operate the Boxcar Grill back in April Springs.

"Hey, Momma, do you have a second?" I asked her when she picked up.

"Did you change your mind about dinner?" she asked me. It was hard not to hear the hope in her voice. Maybe I hadn't been spending enough time with her lately.

"Sorry, we're still in Union Square."

"That's fine then. How may I help you?"

"I was wondering if you'd heard anything about Gary Shook selling the strip mall where For The Birds is, or was, I guess I should say."

"I haven't, but that doesn't mean that it's not true," she replied. "If it's important to you, I could make some inquiries."

"If you can do it discreetly, that would be great," I said.

"I am the very model of caution," she replied, chiding me a bit as she said it.

I decided to let it slide. After all, not everything was worth an argument. "Could selling it off explain why he jacked up the rent on all of his tenants? Jenny's not the only one moving on."

"Yes, that could be true. If the buyer wants the property but not the rental income or even the buildings themselves, that could account for it," she replied. "I'm not sure why anyone would want that particular piece of land, though. I have plots of land around town for sale that wouldn't require the investment of having the old buildings torn down."

"You'll look into it though, right?"

"I will," she said. "Are there any holdouts that you know of?"

"Lawrence Grimes appeared to be ready to fight him on it," I admitted.

"Then I'd speak with him again if I were you," she advised. "If Gary was trying to get him out and his presence was holding up the deal, it could have led to an argument, which could have led to much more."

"We'll check that out," I answered. "Thanks for the tip."

"Suzanne, I'm sure you and Grace would have thought of it soon enough. Have you spoken to Jake about what happened today?"

"No, but we're going to check in tonight. I'll tell him then."

"Will he come home to help you?" she asked me. Momma had a great deal of faith in my husband, not that he didn't merit it, but she knew full well that I was perfectly capable of handling this without him.

"He would, but I wouldn't ask," I said. "He's got a job to do at the moment, and he's spending time with his family, too. I wouldn't dream of pulling him back here."

"Never forget that you're his family too, Suzanne," Momma said, as though I needed to be reminded of it.

"So are you," I said, "but Jake is right where he needs to be at the moment, and so am I. Thanks again for your help."

"You're welcome," she said.

Before she could say anything else, I added quickly, "Bye," and I hung up.

"What was that all about?" Grace asked me when I saw that she was looking at me oddly.

"Momma's going to help us figure out what's going on with Gary Shook's property," I said.

"I gathered that much. I'm talking about the last bit."

"She thinks I need Jake here," I told her with a frown.

"Cut her some slack, Suzanne," Grace said with a sympathetic smile. "She means well."

"If I accepted that excuse for her behavior, I'd have an ulcer," I told her. "Besides, I thought you had my back."

"Forever and always," she said quickly. "Are you ready to take a trip to Italy?"

"For the food? You bet. The real thing? Someday maybe. I've got it on my list," I said.

"What's stopping you?" Grace asked me as we pulled into Napoli's parking lot. I was heartened to see that it was nearly full, happy for the DeAngelis women. I knew that even if the dining room was packed or even over capacity, there would always be a place for us back in the kitchen. Honestly, I preferred eating back there anyway.

"The time and the money, I guess. Besides that, I'm good to go."

"Just don't let it wait too long," she said.

"I'll see what I can do," I replied. "Now let's eat."

"Can you squeeze us in?" I asked Antonia as I looked around the crowded dining room.

"Of course I can," she said as she studied the room. I took the time to admire the sheer beauty of the young woman. I wasn't sure how much DNA her father had contributed, but she, like her sisters, was her mother's daughter. Any man in the world would be enchanted with her loveliness on first sight, at least until they caught a glimpse of her mother. Angelica had something besides just beauty. There was a spark in her, a magnet that drew people to her like magic. "I have a party that's overstayed their welcome. Let me have one second."

I touched her arm. "Don't throw them out on our account. Would your mother mind if we ate in the kitchen with her?"

"She wouldn't, but she's not here at the moment," Antonia said. "However, I *know* Sophia would love the company."

Grace asked her softly, "Does it bother any of you at all that your youngest sister has taken over the kitchen and not one of you?"

Antonia shook her head and let out a quick sigh. "We are thankful for her every day. She's the *only* one who can come close to matching our mother's gifts there, and in time, Mom herself believes that Sophia will outshine her."

"That's hard to believe," I said. "Angelica is amazing."

"She is," Antonia agreed, "but Sophia brings a reckless creativity to the process that nearly always works out. She has instincts that are beyond her years." Antonia hesitated, and then she added with a smile, "If either of you tell her that I said any of that, I'll deny it until I'm blue in the face. Do we understand each other?"

"We do," I said, matching her smile with one of my own. "Would you mind asking her if we can eat with her?"

"Just go on back. I *know* she'll love it. Besides, she's been riding Maria about her new boyfriend, and I'm sure they could both use a break from each other—if for nothing else, a pair of referees."

"What makes you think they'll behave just because of us?" Grace asked her.

"They need to be distracted," she said. "Trust me, you'll be doing my sisters a favor."

"Okay. Thanks."

"It's *always* our pleasure to see the two of you," she said with a smile, and for a brief instant I saw her mother's sparkle in her own eyes. It was heady stuff; there was no doubt about that.

"May we come in?" I asked as Grace and I walked back into the kitchen where all of the magic happened. "Antonia said that it would be all right."

"It's more than all right," Maria said. "Sophia, pick on them for a change, would you?"

"They're not dating egomaniacs like you are," Sophia said as she waved a sauce-laden spatula at one of her older sisters.

"He's not that bad. Tim's just a little confident, that's all."

"There's confidence, and then there's maniacal self-assurance based on very little," Sophia said with a frown. "You know I'm right."

Maria picked up two plates of spaghetti and looked at us with exasperation. "See if you two can get her off my back, would you?"

"You know I tell you these things because I love you," Sophia said as her sister headed for the door. "You can do better."

"Thanks for the pep talk, Mom," Maria said.

Sophia frowned as she left, and then she turned to us. "Do I really sound like my mother?"

"There are a great many worse people you could emulate in this world," I told her.

"I know that, but come on, I don't *really* sound like her, do I?"

I laughed. "I catch myself doing the very same thing sometimes, repeating something my mother told me when I was younger. It's aggravating, isn't it? The older I get, the smarter she seems to be."

Sophia laughed as well. "Yes, I'm already seeing that. Now tell me. What can I do for you ladies this evening?"

"Is there any chance you'd be willing to feed us back here?" Grace asked. "We'd like to do the Trip for Two Around Italy."

"Absolutely. Sit down," she said, "but I can do better than that. Do you two trust me?"

"With food or something else?" I asked her with a smile.

"Food," she replied promptly. If she was offended by my question, she didn't show it, but then again, I'd known Sophia most of her life.

"Of course," I said as Grace chimed in as well.

"Excellent. I've been wanting to try something, but I haven't had anyone brave...I mean adventurous enough to experiment on," she answered with a wicked little chuckle.

"Experiment away," Grace replied. "If you make it, I'll eat it."

"You don't know what you've gotten yourself into," she said with a laugh, "but you'll love it. I promise you."

"Bring it on then," I answered.

Chapter 10

IT WAS ONE OF THE MOST unique and imaginative concoctions of food that I'd ever had in my life, there was no doubt about that. Sophia started us off with a homemade grilled cheese sandwich that was so much more than that mundane description. Instead of using regular old American cheese like the ones I always made, Sophia had concocted a blend of cheeses and herbs that complemented each other amazingly well, wedged and melted between two pieces of grilled and buttered garlic toast that crunched with crispness with each bite. Calling it a grilled cheese sandwich was disrespectful to the sandwich Grace and I split.

The young chef had been watching us closely, and as she turned to fill another of Maria's orders, I asked, "Are you ready for your report card so far?"

She laughed. "I don't need one. I saw the way you two devoured that sandwich. I'm going to ask Mom to put it on our lunch menu. I was thinking about pairing it with some tomato soup that will knock your socks off, but I haven't gotten that recipe quite right yet."

"Would you like some advice?" I asked her.

"From you? Always," she replied.

"Wait until you've perfected that too and then present them together to your mother. I already know how amazing it's going to be."

"That's a good note," she said. "Now I'm going to feed you both a twist on pasta I've been playing with that I have high hopes for."

As she threw together sampler after sampler for us, I found myself in awe of her ability to take mostly the same basic ingredients and turn them into such special and individual tasty foods. "You're pretty amazing," I said as we finished her new spin on tiramisu that was a distant cousin of the original but delightful in its own way.

"How's that? I mean, I know that you're right, but what makes you say that at the moment?" Sophia asked me with a broad smile.

"You make so many deliciously unexpected things from tried-and-true ingredients. Don't you ever run out of ideas?"

"Said the donut lady who offers a hundred different donut flavors in her shop," Sophia said. "That's what's amazing to me."

"It's only fifty at last count," I said with a grin.

"Still, I doubt I'd be able to come up with even a dozen."

"I think you'd probably surprise yourself," I told her. As I pushed the last plate away, I asked, "What do we owe you?"

"I'm invoking our tasting rule," Sophia said. "Don't argue with me; there wasn't a thing I served you tonight that was on the menu. It's one of my mother's rules, so don't make me tell her that you've been breaking them."

"Where is your mother, by the way?" I asked.

"She went clothes shopping, if you can believe it. We never used to be able to get her out of the kitchen, but now that she's started dating your mayor, she's a ghost around here."

"You don't mind her seeing someone, do you?" I asked.

"Are you kidding? We're all thrilled about it. Mom has never been this happy as far as I'm concerned, and that includes when Dad was still alive. I loved that man dearly, but the two of them expressed their love and affection for each other at some pretty high volumes. With George, there's a peaceful tranquility to the relationship that I hope I find someday myself."

"I'm sure you will," I said.

"If I ever get out of the kitchen, maybe," she answered with a grin as Antonia came back.

"Oh good, you're both still here," the older sister said.

"Where else would we be?" I asked.

"I was afraid you might have slipped out the back," she said. "Someone's out front who wants to speak with you."

"Who is it?" Grace asked. "And how did they even know we were here?"

"Suzanne, your Jeep is pretty distinctive," she said.

"Maybe so, but that still doesn't tell us who wants to talk to us," I said.

"It's Cynthia Logan," she said. "Do you want to see her, or should you slip out the back door?"

Cynthia Logan was the woman from the bank Gary Shook had threatened, at least according to Momma. She was a good customer of mine, especially in the autumn months, when her favorite spice, cinnamon, was in just about everything, or so it seemed to me at times. I'd known her for years, but she hadn't been working at the bank all that long. Why did she want to speak with us tonight? Was there something she needed to tell us about Gary Shook that wouldn't wait until morning? I had a few questions for her myself, but I was going to wait to see what she had to say first before I started in on mine. "We'll go out through the dining room and have a chat with her," I told her. "Thanks for looking out for us, though."

"You're most welcome," Antonia said.

Before we walked out front though, I turned back to Sophia. "Are you sure we can't pay you for that wonderful meal?"

"I'm sure," she said. "Your feedback is all that I was looking for."

"It was all amazing. Is that what you needed?" Grace asked her with a smile.

"I was hoping for something a little more specific than that, but I'll take what I can get," Sophia answered with a grin of her own.

"We'll get back to you," I told her, and I meant it.

"No worries," Sophia answered as Maria walked back into the kitchen with an empty tray.

"For some reason I can't fathom, the party at table seven want to give their compliments to the chef, Sophia."

"Ladies, I'd love to stay and chat, but apparently, my adoring public awaits," Sophia said with a flourish.

"I wouldn't get too excited about it," Maria told her little sister. "I'm not one hundred percent sure they've ever eaten out in a restaurant before."

"Then think how lucky they were to come here tonight for their first experience," she said.

All three girls laughed, and as Grace and I walked out of the kitchen into the dining room, we saw the bank loan officer waiting for us by the door.

"Hey, Suzanne. Do you have a second?" Cynthia Logan asked me. Sometimes it was easy to forget how tall and shapely she was, but it was even more obvious than usual when I was standing right beside her.

"Sure, but let's go outside," I said. I didn't want our conversation to distract from anyone's dining experience.

Grace nodded her approval, and the three of us walked out the door. I glanced back at the last second and saw Sophia taking her well-earned bow. It was indeed food worthy of praise, and I was glad that folks were appreciating the flair and the care that she put into it. I couldn't blame Angelica for spending more time away from the restaurant when she had a substitute so capable of running the place in her absence. I felt the same way about Emma and Sharon. On the days when they worked at Donut Hearts without me, I *knew* that my customers were getting goodies every bit as delightful as the ones I made for them. It was the only way I could justify being away.

"What's so urgent that you needed to see me tonight?" I asked her.

She looked puzzled. "I never said that it was urgent. I saw your Jeep outside, so I asked Antonia where you were, since I didn't see you in the dining room."

"We were in the kitchen," I said. "Have you ever met Grace Gauge?"

"Yes," Grace said as Cynthia said, "No," at the same time.

The loan officer looked puzzled. "I'm sorry. Have we met?"

"At Sally Wright's Halloween party last year," Grace said. "It's okay if you don't remember me. I was in costume."

"What were you wearing?"

"I was a troll," Grace replied.

"That's right," she said. "I loved your keyboard and screen."

I remembered that costume, too. Grace had come as an internet troll, complete with gnarly warts, green makeup, and a homemade computer setup. She always did come up with the best outfits.

"Thanks," she said.

"If it wasn't that important, why did you want to see me? Did you just want to say hi?" We had never been that close; she was just another customer with a very specific set of tastes. I had some who only bought apple fritters, some with a passion for chocolate éclairs, and some, like Cynthia, with a hankering for a certain spice.

"When are you going to make the triple-cinnamon donuts again?" she asked. "I bought four dozen last winter and froze what I couldn't eat, but I ran out last week."

Those donuts had been for customers with a very selective palate indeed. I'd mixed cinnamon in with the cake donut dough, piped them full of a vanilla cinnamon filling, and doused them in enough cinnamon to choke a horse, not that I'd ever have any interest in doing that to a horse, or anyone else for that matter. I remembered the batch in particular Cynthia had raved about, and she'd bought me out of them. "I'm not sure if they'll make it to the menu again, but if they do, it probably won't be until October," I said.

Her frown was apparent. "I see. That's too bad."

"She can always do special runs, though," Grace piped up. "What's the minimum for those, Suzanne?"

"Three dozen," I told her.

"Let me think about it," Cynthia said. "What brings you two to Union Square? Did you come all this way just to eat at Napoli's?"

"We had some other business in town, too," Grace said, which was more than I would have shared with the loan officer. Since Grace and I had become known for investigating murder on occasion in the area, I usually liked to downplay our activities, but maybe I was just being a bit too paranoid. Then again, it would be the perfect opportunity to ask her about her recent confrontation with Gary Shook.

"You must have been shocked to hear what happened to Gary Shook," I said.

"I was surprised, that's true enough, but I don't know that I was all that shocked by the news. Gary had a way of putting people on edge, didn't he?"

"That's right," I said, pretending to remember what Momma had told me. "The two of you had a fight a few days ago, didn't you?"

"A fight? No, not that I recall," she said as she looked a bit puzzled.

"Really? That's odd. I heard it from a reliable witness that you two were going at it in your office," I pushed.

It suddenly dawned on her who my source was. "Your mother told you. Of course she did. It was nothing," Cynthia said.

"What was it about?" Grace asked curiously.

"He wanted an extension on one of his loans, but I'd already pushed it sixty days, and I was getting heat from my boss to foreclose on the loan."

"Really? I was under the impression that Gary had inherited a load of money from someone in his family," I said.

"I really shouldn't talk about it," she said as she bit her lower lip.

"There's no real assumption of confidentiality now that he's dead, is there?" I asked her.

Cynthia thought about it for a second and then said, "I suppose it's going to be public knowledge soon enough, anyway. Gary blew through that money six months ago. He was in debt up to his eyebrows, and now that he's gone, I'm guessing the bank is going to be on the hook for those properties. I'm probably going to lose my job because someone killed him."

"Is it really that dire?" I asked her. I felt bad for anyone who was facing the prospect of being out of work. That was one of the best things about being self-employed. I might not always like my boss, but she was stuck with me, and she couldn't fire me.

"Probably, but I've been thinking about getting out of the banking business anyway."

"What will you do instead?" I asked.

She shrugged. "I don't know, but I'll figure something out when the time comes. I'll get back to you about that special order."

"You do that," I said as she got into her vehicle, a nice BMW, and drove off.

"That's a pretty fancy ride for someone about to be canned," Grace said.

"It's probably a lease," I told her.

"Either that or she gave herself a loan at a killer rate," Grace said.

"That's kind of cold, isn't it?" I asked her as we walked over to my Jeep. "Don't tell me you're angry she didn't remember meeting you last year."

"Of course not," Grace said. "What do you take me for, a petulant child? It was a great costume, though."

"I thought so, too," I said.

As we drove back to April Springs, Grace took out her cell phone.

"Who are you calling?"

"I'm not," she said as she tapped a few keys.

"Okay, texting then," I said.

"I'm not doing that, either. I'm making a list of suggestions for Sophia," she answered. "After all, she was nice enough to feed us, and we did promise."

"That's a great idea, but do you really have any ideas as to how she could improve that magnificent meal?"

Grace shrugged. "I have a few suggestions."

"Tell them to me as you're typing," I suggested.

"Okay, I thought the grilled cheese sandwiches could have really used some ham."

"If she'd done that, they wouldn't have been grilled cheese sandwiches, would they?" I asked her.

"No, but they would have been even better in my book," Grace said.

"I thought there was too much garlic in the butter she used to grill the bread, myself," I admitted.

"You're right," Grace said as she kept typing. "I'd forgotten all about that. "Anything else?"

"I might have liked a little more sauce with the stuffed ziti," I said. "Plus, what was that mix she used inside of them? I loved the ricotta, the Parmesan, and the mozzarella, but that cheddar clashed with *everything*. I know she's trying to be edgy, but that flavor didn't match the others. It was a rare misstep for her."

"You ate it anyway though, didn't you?" she asked me with a grin.

"Neither one of us left a morsel behind," I reminded her.

"True. Anything else?"

"No, that does it. How do we tell her?" I asked. "Should we turn around and go back to the restaurant so we can do it in person?" I hated the idea of adding another hour to my evening of driving, but Sophia deserved to hear our comments face-to-face. I regretted not telling her what we'd thought while we'd been there, and I promised myself that if we ever served as tasters for her again, we'd give her our honest opinions on the spot, no matter what. That was the only way we were going to be able to avoid the sinking feeling I was having now about how to tell a dear friend *anything* that she might not want to hear.

Chapter 11

"YOU CAN DROP ME OFF at my place if you're planning to do that, but I'm not going back to Union Square," Grace said. "Let's just call her and get it over with."

"Seriously? Now?"

"We both know we can't send her a text or an email, Suzanne. Sophia will never know how much we really loved just about everything she fed us tonight if she can't hear it in our voices."

That was a fair point. We were just coming into April Springs, so I pulled off in front of the bank. "You know, there's a good chance she might not even be free."

"If she's not, then we'll do it tomorrow, but I'm *never* going to let this happen again. We tell her on the spot or we don't do it at all. Agreed?"

"I was just thinking the exact same thing myself," I admitted.

I wasn't sure I wanted to *ever* have this particular conversation, but we'd been asked, so we were under an obligation to do it, no matter how uncomfortable it might be.

I had to admit though that I was kind of hoping she wouldn't be free to talk to us. I put the phone on speaker just in case and dialed her number.

Too bad for us, Sophia picked up on the second ring. "What's going on? Do you two miss me already?" she asked.

"We know you're busy, but when you get a chance, we'd like to talk to you about the menu tonight," I said.

"There's no rush, though," Grace piped up.

"As a matter of fact, I'm off now. Momma came back raring to get into the kitchen, and she practically threw me out into the street. I'm all yours, so talk to me, ladies."

"First of all, it's important that you know how much we loved ninety-eight percent of that meal," I said. "It was magical."

"Truly amazing," Grace added.

"If I want blind acceptance and unconditional love, I'll get a dog," Sophia said. "I want the two percent that *wasn't* a home run."

"Okay, this probably isn't even a thing," Grace said, "but I thought that grilled cheese sandwich could have used some shaved ham."

"I thought about doing that. Actually, I would have made it a croque monsieur, but Mom would have never stood for it. That was as close as I could get without her objecting."

"Why, doesn't she like French cooking?" I asked.

"She loves it, as long as it's Italian," Sophia said with a chuckle, "but I'll consider it. What else did you not like?"

"There was a bit too much garlic in the buttered bread for the grilled cheese sandwich for my taste, and then there was the stuffed ziti," I said.

Before I could even go into more detail, Sophia said, "The cheddar clashed in it, didn't it? I knew it."

"A little bit," I confessed.

"Come on, it was like wearing a wedding dress with combat boots. I knew in my gut it was a mistake, but I did it anyway. Thanks for verifying it for me. What's next?"

We mentioned a few other small details, and Sophia laughed when we finished with our list.

"What's so funny?" I asked her.

"You were *much* too easy on me," she said. "Mom would have had seven complaints about the sandwich alone, and my sisters might not have liked something, but they wouldn't have been able to tell me why. You two more than earned your free meals tonight."

"So, we're all good?" I asked her. It was vitally important to my well-being that I be on good terms with the entire DeAngelis clan. They were very much a second family to me.

"Better than good, we're great. Listen, I may call you both next week when I'm ready to test a few more choices. Are you game?"

"I think we could squeeze you into our busy schedules," I said with a laugh.

"If Suzanne can't make it, at least I'll be there," Grace added, joining in.

"Thanks, I appreciate that. Good night, ladies."

"Good night," we chimed out in unison.

After we hung up and I started driving toward Grace's place, I said, "That went well."

"Did you expect something else?" she asked me as I parked my Jeep in front of her home and shut off the engine.

"Most folks are sensitive when you criticize their food, and chefs are notoriously bad at hearing constructive comments," I said.

"Well, she did ask us for our honest opinions," Grace reminded me.

"I know, but I'm still glad everything's still good between us."

"You hate having anyone upset with you, don't you?" she asked me. "You always have."

"Who doesn't like to be liked?" I asked her. "Besides you, I mean," I answered with a grin.

"I like it when people like me. I just don't *require* it," she replied. "Suzanne, as much as it pains me to say, I'd love to hang out and chat with you, but I've got a ton of paperwork to wade through tonight. Are you running the donut shop tomorrow?"

"Yes, Emma's helping me, and then she and her mother have it for the two days after that," I said.

"Then we'll start digging again after you close the donut shop?" she asked.

"If you can make the time, I'd love to have your help," I said.

"I'll be there," she answered.

After I dropped Grace off at her place, I decided to give Jake a call. It wasn't exactly early for me, but it wouldn't be too much longer before

I had to go to bed. It was one of the major inconveniences of owning a donut shop, but I'd mostly gotten used to the hours. The problem was that I hadn't been able to adjust my sleep schedule very well on the days I was off, so I was constantly yawning at the most inopportune times, even when I wasn't due to get up early the next morning.

I drove the rest of the way home and sat on the porch swing in front of our cottage before I made the call.

"Hey, have a second?" I asked Jake when he picked up.

"Sure. For you I can spare five or six," he said with a slight chuckle.

It always amazed me how good it was just to hear his voice. "How goes the investigation?"

"It's slow, but at least it's giving me a chance to catch up here," he said.

"How's that going?"

"I don't know," he said with a sigh. "You know my sister and her kids. It seems as though one of them is in trouble all of the time. I wish I could do more for them, but it's tough being so far away."

"I know you miss them," I answered sympathetically. Jake could run his consulting business anywhere, and the only real ties he had to April Springs were to me. On the other hand, it felt as though my entire existence was here. I felt guilty about it at times, but not guilty enough to chuck everything and move to Raleigh. I was a mountain kind of girl, and between Donut Hearts, Momma, and all of my friends, I couldn't imagine ever leaving.

"I do, but it will be all right. Brighten my mood and tell me about your day. Did you have any wacky customers? Hang on a second, today was that big sale for your friend. How did that go?"

"As a matter of fact, it went great. She cleaned out her inventory and made enough besides that to help her start over, but something else happened."

"What?" Jake asked keenly.

"Somebody killed Gary Shook in the For The Birds storeroom," I said.

"I don't know him. What happened?"

Sometimes I forgot that Jake wasn't local. He blended in so well with the citizenry of April Springs that it was hard to imagine there had ever been a time when he hadn't lived there, let alone been such a crucial part of my life. "He was her landlord, and someone stabbed him in the chest," I said.

"Jenny didn't do it, did she?"

"I don't *think* so, but no one knows for sure just yet. Evidently Gary slipped in through the back, and as far as we can tell, someone must have followed him in, stabbed him, and then got away clean without anyone seeing them."

"Did they find the knife?" Jake asked.

"It wasn't a knife. It was a decorative flag holder," I said.

"I thought those things were really flimsy," he commented.

"They usually are, but Jenny bought a bunch that were beefier than what you'd usually expect. It was more than enough to do the job," I said as I shivered a bit from the recent memory of it sticking straight up out of his chest.

There was a momentary pause before my husband asked, "Suzanne, are you involved in this somehow?"

"Grace and I were the ones who found him, Jake," I admitted. "We were going to try to stay out of it anyway, but Jenny needs our help. I didn't want for this to happen, but we can't just walk away."

"I get that," Jake said. "Listen, I'd love to come home and help, but I kind of have my hands full at the moment." He took a deep breath and then continued, "But if you need me, I can be there in four hours. *You're* my top priority. Everyone else will just have to find a way to get by without me."

"It's sweet of you to offer, but Grace and I have this under control," I said. I wasn't at all sure that was true, but what else could I say? I wasn't about to have Jake leave his obligations in Raleigh just to come home and hold my hand.

"Are you sure?" he asked, and unless I was mistaken, he sounded a little bit relieved.

"I'm positive," I said.

"Okay then, but if things change and you need me, I'm there for you."

"I know, and I can't tell you how much I appreciate that," I said.

"Uncle Jake, are you coming back?" I heard someone ask from the other room.

"You've got to go," I said. "We'll talk again soon."

"Tomorrow," Jake promised. "Watch your back, lady. I don't want anything to happen to you."

"That goes double for you," I said.

After we hung up, I thought about going inside, but I just wasn't ready for bed yet, no matter how much my body protested that was a lie. I decided to take a stroll around the park before I settled in for the evening, so I left the porch and walked toward the Boxcar Grill. I didn't have room for even the tiniest sliver of pie or cake, but that didn't mean that I couldn't check in with my friend there.

And if she offered me a little something, it would be rude to say no.

At least that was what I was going to tell myself if it came up.

"I can't believe you ate dinner at Napoli's and then had the nerve to come here," Trish said after I'd greeted her.

"What? How did you know that? Was Grace here?"

"No, but you've got a little marinara sauce on your shirt, and I know Napoli's is the only place you'll eat Italian cuisine," she said with a grin, her mock severity gone. "How was it?"

"Would it ruin our friendship forever if I said that it was amazing?" I asked her with a smile.

"No. It might damage it a little, but I'm a big person. I'll find a way to get over it."

"It was okay," I said, doing my best to suppress a smile.

"Suzanne, don't you dare lie to me. I want details," she replied.

"Sophia tried out some new menu items on us," I told her. "That girl's got some natural talent."

"I'm sure that she does, but it doesn't hurt being trained by someone like Angelica DeAngelis. That woman has it all, doesn't she?"

"Including our mayor," I said and then realized I probably shouldn't have said that. Even though they'd made a rather public appearance together earlier that day, I wasn't sure that it was common knowledge yet in April Springs that they were dating. If they *were* still trying to keep a low profile, I'd probably just blown it for them. "Trish, don't spread that around, okay? I'm not sure I should have even mentioned it."

"Hadn't you heard? He brought her here on a date three nights ago," she said with a smile. "They aren't exactly the perfect match on paper, but they seem to be making it work. Good for them," she said with a wistful shrug.

"How's your love life?" I asked.

"It was a bit warm out today, wasn't it?" she asked. "I thought it might rain in the morning, but it cleared up nicely for the big sale." Her point was that she didn't want to discuss it, so I dropped it.

"Just out of curiosity, what's for dessert tonight?"

"Are you seriously still peckish after eating at Napoli's?" she asked me.

"Not really, but Jake is out of town, and I don't feel like being alone." The honest rawness of my comment caught me off guard, and Trish seemed surprised as well.

"Then you came to the right place," she said. "We've got caramel apple pie, apple glazed tarts, and apple upside down cake."

"I'm sensing a trend here," I said.

"Hilda just started dating a guy from Brushy Mountain who owns an orchard," she said softly. "We're drowning in apples, but I don't have the heart to tell her to make something else. She's been begging me to put some of it on the menu, and today I finally relented."

"What's the consensus been so far?"

"Everybody wants us to keep it coming," she said. "You know Hilda. She could make *any* ingredient work. So, do any of those choices tempt you?"

"They all do, but I guess I'll just go with the pie tonight." I looked around and spotted my friend, Paige Hill, from The Last Page bookshop. "I'll be over there."

"Do you want some coffee to go with that?" she asked.

"No, it will probably just keep me up. I'll have sweet tea instead."

Trish looked at me oddly. "That's got caffeine in it too, you know."

"I understand that, but Southern sweet tea is like mother's milk to me. If ever I was in the need of something that gave me comfort, it's now."

"Coming right up," she said.

I walked over to Paige's table, and she smiled when she saw me. "You're up late, aren't you?"

I glanced at my watch. "I've got plenty of time before bed," I said. "At least half an hour, anyway. Want some company?"

"You? Always. Where's Grace?" she asked me as I sat down.

"Doing paperwork at home. Besides, we're not *always* together."

"I know that, but when you two are digging into murder, you're virtually inseparable."

"Are we that obvious?"

"Maybe not to someone who doesn't know you," she said as Trish showed up. Paige had finished her meal, and she looked at the plate I had delivered with clear envy. Instead of just the pie I'd asked for, there were half portions of all *three* of the apple-based desserts Trish had told me about earlier. "What did you order, Suzanne? I didn't see a sampler on the menu."

"It's the house special for this table, one night only," Trish said. "Want one?"

"I probably shouldn't," Paige said. "But if I only did what I should, think how boring life would be. Why not?"

"I'll bring it right up," Trish said.

"I didn't even realize that I'd ordered this special," I told the Boxcar Grill owner.

"What can I say? Sometimes the customer *doesn't* know best. If you're not happy about it though, give it to Paige and I'll get you what you asked for, not what you really wanted."

"Thanks, but I don't want to put you to any trouble," I said as I slid the plate a little closer to me.

"I appreciate that," Trish said.

"You can join us, you know," I offered.

"I would if I could, but I've got to talk some sense into Hilda. She wants to put *more* apples on our menu, and I'm afraid I'm going to have to put my foot down."

"Good luck with that," I said.

A moment later, Trish brought Paige her sampler as well, and we dug in. It had taken every last bit of my willpower not to attack it the moment it was in front of me, but I wanted to see if I could show restraint when faced with so much temptation.

I managed it, but just barely.

As we both sampled our plates, Paige asked me, "How's the investigation going?"

"You know how these things go," I told her. "At first it's a muddled mess and we're just looking for pieces that fit into the puzzle. It's not until we've almost got it that things start to come together."

"So, it's not like most of the mysteries we've both read," she said. Paige was as big a fan of cozies as I was, and we often had our own little impromptu book club meetings with just the two of us. The group I'd belonged to earlier had broken up, once and for all, I was afraid. At least

I think that was what had happened. They'd stopped coming to Donut Hearts, and my texts were mostly met with brief replies about when we might get together again. Murder had come between my three friends and me, and though I hated the fallout from one of my investigations, I'd had to do what I'd done. It was just one more casualty of the particular avocation I'd chosen for myself inadvertently. I wasn't ready to give up on them yet, though. Maybe I'd reach out to the group one more time. After all, all they could do was reject me again, and while I'd never get used to it, I couldn't let it stop me.

"Suzanne, did I lose you just then?" Paige asked, interrupting my bleak thoughts.

"Sorry, I was just thinking about something else," I told her.

"Was it Gary Shook?" she asked softly, though we just about had the diner to ourselves, at least our section of it at any rate.

"That too, but mostly I was thinking about some old friends I haven't seen in much too long," I told her honestly.

"You should get in touch with them," Paige said decisively. "They're probably too afraid to reach out to you themselves."

"I've tried, but they don't seem to be all that receptive these days," I said, and then I knew that I had to change the subject. It wasn't fair to dump my burdens onto Paige. "How did your part of the sale go?"

"We raised a little under two hundred dollars," she said. "All in all, it wasn't bad, given the circumstances."

"Yes, Gary Shook's murder kind of took the wind out of all of our sails," I admitted.

"And killed our sales, too," Paige said. "Sorry about that. This is not a good time for puns."

"Is there *ever* a good time for them, though?" I asked her with a slight grin.

"I admit I enjoy a little wordplay now and then," Paige said.

"I do too, but don't tell anybody else."

"Your secret is safe with me," she said. "I wish I could say that I was surprised that someone killed Gary, but I'm not. He certainly wasn't a very good guy."

"He clearly had his moments," I said. "I know you told Grace and me about dating him once, but is there anything *else* about him I don't know that you haven't told us?"

"How can I possibly answer that question?" she asked me with a shrug. "For me to do that, I'd have to know everything you know."

"That's fair," I said. "I know you had your own set of problems with him, but is there any *other* reason you didn't like him?"

Paige played with a bit of cake on her plate. She had shown remarkable restraint, leaving portions of each selection, while I'd cleaned my plate so thoroughly that it barely needed to be run through the dishwasher. "That's kind of the problem. I'm not sure it's my story to tell."

"I can respect that," I told her, "but if it will help us find a killer, isn't that what's really important?"

"I can trust you, right?" she asked.

"If you have to ask, I'm not sure you should," I told her honestly.

"I know I can," Paige replied. "What I'm about to tell you makes it even worse that I actually went out with that thug later. I'm afraid you're not going to think very kindly of me once you hear what happened."

I reached out and touched her hand. "Paige, I married an unscrupulous actor who cheated on me, so I'm certainly not going to judge you for your choice in men."

"Okay, if you're sure. A friend of mine from Union Square dated him in high school, and he was bad news even back then."

"In what way?"

"All she would tell me at the time was that she went out on a date with him that ended badly, and by the time it was over, she was walking home alone, and his face at school the next day looked as though he'd lost a fight with a herd of cats. He'd told me that he'd changed when I asked him about it, but clearly he'd lied to me."

Apparently this leopard hadn't changed his spots at all since then, based on the way he'd tried to coerce Molly into doing something she wasn't comfortable doing. That suggested a lifelong pattern to me, and I had to wonder if he'd pushed the wrong woman this time, just as he had in high school. This time, she might have fought back with something quite a bit more deadly than her fingernails. If that had been the case, was I really all that eager to find out who had killed the man? The truth was that I still had a job to do, and that was to get Jenny off the hook. If Gary Shook's murderer had also been his victim, then I'd turn the tables and do everything in my power to help her, but in the meantime, Jenny needed me more. Besides that, there were more suspects on our list that had their own motives to want to see the landlord dead.

"Suzanne, I can call her if you'd like to hear her side of the story directly. Is that why you've been so quiet?"

"No, I've just been thinking about what I know about the man and how this fits into the puzzle. There's no reason to make your friend relive such a painful part of her life, Paige. You've helped just by telling me her story, so there's no reason to involve her at this point."

"You've got a good heart, my friend."

"When the very word is in your name, you kind of have to," I told her with a grin.

"I don't think that's true at all," she said. "I know quite a few folks who don't match their names one bit."

"Are we talking personally, or maybe authors? Because we both know a great many writers use pseudonyms these days."

"They've been doing it as long as there have been published stories," she said.

"Would you?" I asked her.

"Would I what? Use a pen name if I wrote something? I wouldn't want to, but I understand the rationale behind it, at least from the publisher's perspective."

"That doesn't answer my question," I pushed.

She gave it a bit of thought and then sighed before she spoke again. "If it meant the difference between being able to tell my stories and not being able to, I'd swallow just about anything they forced me to, especially in the bad old days."

"When exactly were the bad old days?" I asked her.

"Before writers could skip publishers altogether and produce their work independently."

"That's an odd point of view coming from a bookseller," I told her.

"I don't think so. We have to change with the times. Do you know the percentage of small, independent, self-published books I carry these days?"

"I haven't a clue," I admitted.

"You'd be shocked if I told you the number, and it's growing every day. I like keeping a balance between the old and the new, but I'm afraid if we don't embrace the changes in our industry, it's going to leave us behind." Paige shook her head gently. "And that is the end of today's lecture. Don't forget, your term papers are due on Friday, and the midterm is going to account for half of your grade, so go home and study!"

"Yes, Ms. Hill," I said with a smile.

"Has anyone ever told you that you're easy to talk to, Suzanne?" Paige asked me.

"What can I say? I truly enjoy listening to what people have to say."

"It shows, too. Come over sometime, and I'll introduce you to some new indie writers that are simply amazing."

"I will as soon as things settle down."

Paige grabbed my bill, even though I protested. "That's for the conversation. Don't wait until your life is quiet to come see me. I've got a feeling that's *never* going to happen."

"You're probably right."

Chapter 12

"SO, HOW WAS EVERYTHING?" Trish asked as Paige paid.

"The food was great, but the dessert was absolutely amazing. You should think about adding that sampler to the menu," she said.

"I probably will, if for no other reason than to use it all up," she said with a grin. "You two ladies have a good night."

"You, too," we said.

As we walked out, I asked Paige, "Are you heading home?"

"No, I'm going back to the store," she said as she pointed to her nearby bookstore. "Care to come in and continue our chat?"

"I'd love to, but I have to make donuts bright and early tomorrow morning."

"We're both too dedicated to our work for our own good; you know that, don't you?"

"I suspect that it's true," I told her.

As I walked the short distance back to the cottage I shared with Jake, I decided to text my three book club friends again. It probably wouldn't yield any better results than my last few attempts, but I wasn't going to just give up, at least not yet.

By the time I was ready for bed, there still wasn't any response from them.

Maybe I'd hear from them tomorrow, but for now, I needed my sleep.

As I'd told Paige, it would be time to get up to make the donuts yet again soon enough.

The first thing I did when I woke up the next morning was turn on my phone and check my messages.

I'd been hoping to get a reply from at least one of my fellow book club members, but unfortunately, not a single one of them answered.

There was a nice message from Jake wishing me a good night's rest though, so I took solace in at least that much, that there was someone out there who loved me.

Most days, that was more than enough for me.

I got to the donut shop and quickly forgot about the slight from my old friends. After all, I was in my element again, making donuts and shutting out the rest of the world, even the sordid one Gary Shook had created for himself. Flipping on switches on the coffee urn and the deep fryer seemed to turn a switch on in me as well, and I found myself happier than I'd been in days just compiling the ingredients for today's donuts. On a whim, even though we were in late summer, I decided it was the perfect time to make a surprise batch of pumpkin cake donuts and some triple-cinnamon donuts for Cynthia as well, just in case she came by the shop. After the batters were all mixed for the cake donuts, I began filling my dropper and placing rounds directly into the hot oil, flipping them halfway through the frying process. I knew that some donut shops, especially the big chains, had automated just about every step of their process, but I took great pride in what I did, and when a donut didn't come out perfectly, it wasn't rejected. Instead, I put it out for sale just like all of its more perfect sisters. No one had ever complained to me that their donut wasn't pretty enough. Besides, I operated on such a razor-thin margin that I couldn't exactly afford to reject any donuts that weren't perfectly shaped. Still, even if I'd made enough to get by without them, I still would have offered them to the world just as they were.

Emma came in and smiled as she put her apron on. "Pumpkin donuts! Cool! I was craving some the other day when Mom and I were here, and I thought about making a batch, but I wasn't sure you'd be okay with that."

I looked at her oddly as I handed her a freshly glazed pumpkin treat. "You're not serious, are you, Emma?"

"You like things the way you like them," she said with a shrug as she took a bite and then smiled. "Suzanne, these are amazing."

"Some of that is probably because they are so unexpected this time of year," I told her.

"Don't sell yourself too short," she said. "Here, have a bite."

I didn't even hesitate. I took the offered morsel and tasted it. It was indeed delightful, even more so because it was still warm and the glaze hadn't even fully set yet. "Not bad."

"It's a whole lot better than that," she said as she started gathering the dirty pots and pans.

"By the way, I was sorry to hear about your aunt," I told her as I continued to drop more mundane donut flavors into the hot oil. "I only heard about her passing away yesterday morning."

"Thanks. It's been a long time coming. I'll always wonder if she fought too hard in the end, but she's better off now, and Mom came to terms with losing her sister a long time ago."

"Listen, if there's anything I can do, just let me know, okay? I'm here for you."

"Thanks, but it's all wrapped up. Aunt Betty died three days ago. After a quick service, she was cremated, and we spread her ashes on the Blue Ridge Parkway just like she wanted, and her attorney took care of the details of the will while everyone was still around."

"Wow, that was fast," I commented as I pulled out a batch of plain cake donuts from the hot oil with my metal spider and put them on the rack, ready to be glazed.

"Like I said, it wasn't a surprise, and that was my aunt's wish, that we make as little fuss as possible. I used to think I'd like a big funeral, but the older I get, the more I just want folks to remember me the way I was."

"Wise words from a woman barely into her twenties," I said.

"Death has a way of making you reexamine what you're doing with your life," Emma said with a hint of a frown. "Can we talk? I mean later?"

"Always," I said. "Can it wait for our break?"

"Yeah, actually, that would probably be better."

"Do you mind if I ask what our topic is going to be?" I asked her.

"It should wait," she said.

"Good enough," I replied as I finished my glazing. I had three more batches of cake donuts to go, and then it would be time to mix the yeast donut dough, the first stage in making the second donut type we offered every morning. Everything went smoothly as I finished the cake donuts, and Emma washed the dishes in mostly silence as I started adding ingredients to our large stand mixer. I didn't even try to draw her out. Mainly that was because I was afraid of what she was about to tell me. My assistant and friend had talked about leaving Donut Hearts for quite a while, and I understood the impulse completely.

I just hoped that it wasn't going to be sooner rather than later.

As I covered the mixer bowl for the yeast dough's first rising, I turned to Emma. "Are you ready for our break?"

She glanced at the wall clock. "Can it wait a few minutes?"

Suddenly she wasn't in such a hurry to talk to me anymore? "I'd love to push it, but you know that dough. It waits for no woman."

"Okay, fine," Emma said as she dried her hands on a towel and followed me outside.

The humidity was down as a change of pace, and there was a gentle breeze blowing outside, swirling and shifting the night air into something almost pleasant. I could smell rain in the air, but it wasn't there yet, so we had a beautiful dark morning to enjoy together.

I just wasn't so sure that the lovely weather was going to be enough to offset whatever it was that Emma was about to tell me.

"What is it? What's going on with you?" I asked her as I took my seat at our outdoor table. "You know that you can tell me anything."

"I was just really hoping...great. Here she is," she finished as a familiar car drove up and parked in front of Donut Hearts. Emma's mother, Sharon, got out and joined us.

"Sorry I'm late," she said.

"How can you be late when I wasn't expecting you at all?" I asked her. "I was sorry to hear about your sister."

"Thanks," Sharon said absently and then turned to her daughter. "Did you ask her yet?"

"I was waiting for you," Emma said.

"Well, I'm here, so go on. If you're sure this is what you want, anyway."

Emma nodded. "I'm sure. How about you?"

"I'm all for it," Sharon said.

"Would someone mind telling me what you're both so sure about?" I asked.

"Suzanne, Mom and I want to buy Donut Hearts," she said, and it was all I could do not to fall off my chair.

Chapter 13

"EXCUSE ME?" I ASKED them, wondering where this had come from.

"Mom and I got a sizable inheritance from Aunt Betty, and her only condition was that we invest in some kind of business. She was an entrepreneur since she was a teenager, and it was something she believed in wholeheartedly."

"And you want to buy my shop?" I asked, still stunned by the news.

"Suzanne, you've been talking about how tough it is to get up every morning, and with Jake's schedule, he's not working all that much these days. If you take our offer, you'll be free to travel, to enjoy life, and to sleep in for a change." Emma bit her thumbnail intermittently as she made her offer as she stared at me, searching for some kind of reaction.

"Is this what you want too, Sharon?" I asked her.

"What I would have loved to do was use the money for travel, but that isn't an option. This will give us both a purpose in life, and we both think of this place as our home away from home."

"Is that even legal, making you buy a business with your inheritance?" I asked, trying to take it all in. Sell Donut Hearts? I couldn't imagine doing it. But then again, it could be an amazing new chapter in my life with Jake. That part of it was certainly tempting.

"I don't know, but it was what Bets wanted, and I'm not about to go against her last wish," Sharon said. "We've put together an all-cash offer that I think you're going to be happy with." She took out a folded piece of paper and handed it to me.

"Should I look at it now or wait until later?" I asked, delicately holding the paper in my hands as though it was about to explode.

"That's up to you," Sharon said.

"At least glance at it," Emma urged me.

I unfolded the paper and looked at the number printed there. "This has to be a mistake."

"Why, is it not enough?" Emma asked me.

"No, that's the problem. It's *way* too generous. You could start your own donut shop with a great deal less than you're offering me."

"Maybe," Sharon said, "but we want it all, including the name. Suzanne, you know us. We'll continue your legacy and always strive to make Donut Hearts a place you'd be proud of."

"I don't know," I said as I kept gazing at the inflated number. "It's a lot to take in."

"We don't need an answer right away," Emma said. "Take a few days to think about it."

"Just a few days?" I asked her.

"Bets asked that we do this within a week of her passing. It was important to her, so it's important to me," Sharon said.

"To us," Emma amended.

"Okay. Give me thirty-six hours. I need to speak with Jake and my mother," I told them.

"That sounds good," Sharon said as she stood. "Now I'm going to leave you two alone. Thanks for listening, Suzanne."

"You bet," I said just as my timer went off. I would have loved the chance to catch my breath a little before I had to dive back into donut-making, but there wasn't going to be time for that. "Are you coming back in?" I asked Emma as I turned back to the front door.

"I'll be with you in a second," she said.

As I started the next phase of the yeast-donut making, I thought about the offer and the idea of leaving Donut Hearts. With their more-than-generous offer, I wouldn't have to work for a long time, maybe forever, given our savings and Jake's pension. I started thinking about the possibilities as I worked, and I barely noticed Emma come back into the kitchen.

The rest of our time together was mostly spent in silence. There was just too much in the air between us at the moment, and I couldn't think of any idle chitchat for the life of me. It was almost a relief when it was finally time to open Donut Hearts and greet my customers, maybe for the last time in my life.

Though my heart was full of anxiety, I did my best to smile as I walked out to unlock the door. After all, if this day was how my customers were going to remember me, I wanted it to be a good experience for them as well as for me.

The last three people I expected to see in the world were standing out front waiting for me when I went to unlock the front door. Hazel, Elizabeth, and Jennifer, my old book club, were all there with smiles as I let them in.

"What are you three doing here?" I asked as I opened the door.

"We came to apologize," Jennifer, a striking redhead and the leader of our group, said.

"Can you ever forgive us?" Hazel, a woman constantly on a diet, asked.

"Suzanne, we miss you," Elizabeth added. She had the *most* reason not to ever want to see me again. After all, there was no doubt in my mind that she associated me with her husband's murder, even though Jake and I had been the ones to solve the crime.

"I miss you all, too," I said as we had ourselves a group hug. After we broke back apart, I said, "I wasn't sure you wanted to have anything to do with me anymore." It was all I could do not to start crying. I hadn't realized just how much I'd felt isolated since our group had just tapered off into nothing.

"We've all been going through our own set of rough patches," Jennifer said, "but that's no excuse for staying out of touch."

"When I didn't hear from any of you last night, I kind of gave up," I admitted.

"That was my fault," Elizabeth said. "I wanted to be sure Hazel and Jennifer felt the same way that I did. I know we can't make up for what's happened in the past, but do you believe in second chances? If you do, we'd like to bring the book club back, starting in two weeks. Meeting at Donut Hearts was the best accident that ever happened to us."

I was about to say yes when I suddenly realized that I might not own the place in two weeks. They must have seen the hesitation in my glance.

"I *knew* we shouldn't have stayed away so long," Hazel said, nearly starting to cry herself. "She doesn't want to be a part of our group anymore, and who can blame her?"

"That's not it at all," I said quickly. "I'd love to rejoin you, but it might not be here. I've had an offer to sell the place, and I'm seriously considering it." I hadn't fully realized just how much I'd been weighing the possibilities of selling Donut Hearts until that very moment, but once I'd said it, I knew that it was true.

"Why would you ever sell this place?" Jennifer asked. "If you need capital, I'm sure we can find a way to keep you afloat for the short term."

"Yes, we've got resources," Hazel added.

"It's not about the money," I said. "I'm tired, and I didn't realize just how tired I was until Emma offered to buy the shop from me. Sleeping in sounds like a real luxury beyond price right now, to be honest with you."

"How did *Emma* come up with the funds to buy you out?" Jennifer asked softly, the savviest financial member of our group.

"She and her mother got a very specific inheritance," I told her. "It can only be used for the purchase of a business, or so I gathered."

"Would you mind if I asked how much the offer is for?" she asked me. "If you're reluctant to share that information, I understand."

"Come on, you three are like family to me," I said as I opened the paper and handed it to her.

Jennifer whistled softly when she saw the number. "Is this legitimate?"

"It is," I said.

"I'm impressed," Jennifer answered.

"I want to see it," Hazel demanded, and as she took the offer, Elizabeth looked over her shoulder. "That's a serious offer. I can see why you'd be tempted by it."

"I haven't answered her yet. I have until tomorrow to say yes or no."

"Wow, she's giving you a deadline?" Hazel asked as she glanced back into the kitchen. I didn't know if Emma was listening, but it wouldn't have surprised me, and to be fair, I hadn't said anything behind her back that I wouldn't have said to her face.

"It's a promise tied in with the inheritance," I answered.

Jennifer frowned. "I'm not sure I can make it happen, but what if I were to come up with a counteroffer for you?"

That surprised me nearly as much as Emma and Sharon's earlier proposition had. "Jennifer, I'm not dying to sell the place."

"I understand, but what if we could put a group of investors together to buy Donut Hearts from you, what would you say? You'd still be in charge, but you wouldn't have any of the financial headaches that come with owning a business."

"Why would you offer to do that?" I asked her. "If you think I need a grand gesture to take you all back, that's a bit excessive."

"It would be strictly business," she said. "My husband mentioned that he and some other investors have been looking for some area businesses to purchase. They aren't even really all that concerned if you make much of a profit. I don't completely understand the rationale, but it could be the perfect answer."

"Can I think about it and get back to you?" I asked.

"Of course you can," she said. "Anyway, that's not why we came. If you want to rejoin our group, we'll find a place to meet if you sell Donut Hearts to Emma. We miss you, not this shop."

"Well, we miss it, too," Hazel admitted. "Do I smell pumpkin?"

"You've got a good nose," I told her with a smile. "How about if I treat you all to some goodies while you're here?"

"We'd love to, but we've got crazy schedules today," Jennifer said. "Rain check?"

"I might not be able to give you one," I said. "How about if I box up some treats for you all to take with you, on the house?"

"We'll take the donuts, but we're paying for them," Elizabeth insisted.

"Suit yourself," I said, not wanting to argue about anything after losing my friends for so long.

As they were leaving with their donuts, Jennifer said, "Think about my offer, Suzanne."

"Are you even able to make it without talking to your husband?" I asked her.

She smiled. "He started his first business with money from my father. I've made sure to have an equal say in the business since."

"Some would say it's more equal than most," Hazel said with a smile.

Jennifer just shrugged.

Before they could go, I stopped each one of them and hugged them tightly again.

"Hey, don't crush my donuts!" Hazel protested mockingly as I held her tightly.

"Trust me, they taste just as good that way," I replied, squeezing her a little tighter.

Once they were gone, I kept waiting for Emma to come out and talk to me about what had just happened, but she stayed in the kitchen for the next few hours. Maybe she'd heard, maybe she hadn't, but now I had *two* decisions to make and not just *one*. Did I want to sell Donut Hearts outright to her and Sharon, or did I want to let Jennifer's husband and her group of investors buy me out and keep me on running the place? I had a third option as well, and that was to do nothing and keep operating as I had been, but I knew that opportunities like this were rare, and if I turned either group down, I'd likely be running Donut Hearts until I collapsed in the kitchen from old age, overwork, and underpay.

It was a lot to chew on, and I wished Jake was home. I'd talk to him about what was going on soon, but I had a feeling that he'd leave the decision up to me. After all, Donut Hearts was mine. I'd worked hard to make it a viable business through some pretty tough times.

Was I willing to give all of that away? Or more importantly, sell it? Whether I walked away or stayed on to manage it, the shop wouldn't be mine anymore either way. Was that such a bad thing, though? No headaches sounded pretty good to me at the moment, and if I could give up my infernal habit of digging into local crimes that didn't involve me, I might just be able to sit back and enjoy the rest of my life. Some folks might think I was too young to retire, but I knew that I'd eventually find something else to do with my life.

Was that what I wanted, though?

I didn't know, and the bad thing was that I was going to have to figure it out pretty soon, or both offers would be gone.

In the meantime, I needed to work with Grace and solve Gary Shook's murder. Otherwise, Jenny would have that homicide hanging over her head for the rest of her life, and I couldn't imagine just sitting by and doing nothing.

It was going to be a busy next few days until I had to make up my mind once and for all, but I had faith in myself.

Who was I kidding? I was going to do my best, but no matter what happened, I had to live with the consequences of my actions one way or the other, and only time would tell if I'd made the right choice.

I couldn't do anything about that just yet though, but I *could* dig in with Grace and try to make something happen soon with our investigation.

And as soon as I closed Donut Hearts for the day—maybe forever—I'd do my very best to do just that.

Chapter 14

"HEY, MOMMA. IT'S NICE to see you here at the shop."

"Don't look so surprised, Suzanne," my mother said as she approached the counter. "I come here more often than you give me credit for."

"I know. It's just that I was thinking about you a few minutes ago, and now here you are. We must have some kind of special bond," I said with a smile.

That softened her instantly. "I'd like to believe that we do," she said. "I have news for you, at least some partial information about what you asked me about yesterday."

I'd nearly forgotten about tapping my mother as a resource. "Did you figure out what was going on with Gary Shook's properties?" I asked her softly.

Maria Humphries was sitting at a nearby sofa, and she was not only a good customer of mine, but she also happened to be one of the biggest gossips in April Springs, and that was saying something.

Momma noticed Maria listening in as well. "It can wait," she answered in kind.

"Hang on a second," I told her. I walked back to the kitchen and asked Emma, "Would you mind watching the front for a few minutes? Momma's here, and I need to talk to her."

"Take all the time you need," my assistant said, not even able to make eye contact with me. It was weird that things were suddenly so awkward with Emma, but we were both clearly feeling the tension between us that had been there ever since she and her mother had offered to buy Donut Hearts.

"Thanks," I said as I walked out of the kitchen.

"Let's go get a breath of fresh air," I said as I touched Momma's arm. "Could I get you a treat before we go?"

"Are those cinnamon cake donuts?" she asked as she pointed to the still nearly full bin of donuts I'd made on a whim. The pumpkin ones were already gone, but I was afraid I was going to be giving away four dozen of the specialty cinnamon donuts when the day was done.

"They are. Would you like six or seven?" I asked hopefully.

"One would be more than sufficient," she said with a hint of laughter in her voice.

"How about Phillip? Would he like some?"

"Let me guess," she said. "You overestimated the demand for them today."

"What can I say? Sometimes I follow my heart instead of my head. I sold out the pumpkin ones already though, so I'm one for two."

"Bag up three for me," she said with a shrug. "I'm sure Phillip will enjoy them."

I threw an extra in the bag for good measure and handed it to Momma as we walked outside. I knew better than to offer her coffee. She'd been limiting her intake lately, allowing herself one small cup with lunch. If I had her willpower, I'd weigh at least thirty pounds less than I did at the moment. The extra weight wasn't directly because I ran a donut shop, but it certainly didn't help. Was that one more check for the "sell" column? I wasn't sure.

Once we were outside, Momma suggested, "Let's find a bench in the park. It's particularly lovely out today, and I believe that heat wave is finally going to break."

"For now," I told her. "I'm afraid we still have a lot of hot weather ahead of us before cool temperatures come back to April Springs."

"I'm afraid you're right," she said. Once we were settled on a bench that overlooked the front of Donut Hearts, Momma said, "Suzanne, I believe your suspicions were correct."

"Which suspicions were those? I've had so many lately it's hard to keep track of them all. Are you talking about the strip mall property?"

"I am," she said. "Someone has been making overtures to buy the entire plot of land and the buildings that stand on it, and from what I've gathered, the offer is for quite a bit more than it should be."

"There must be a lot of that going around lately," I said, thinking about Emma and Sharon's offer.

"Really? I hadn't noticed. Is something happening with you?"

"We'll talk about that in a second," I told her. "Do you have any idea who is behind the offer? Is it still viable now that Gary is dead? And who inherits his properties now that he's not going to be needing them anymore?"

"All good questions, but I'm afraid I have no other answers for you. My sources at the bank as well as at the courthouse are proving to be particularly reticent to share with me at the moment. I should have more for you from both venues tomorrow."

I wasn't even surprised that my mother had spies in two areas of the community that impacted her businesses, the government and the bank. "Do you have any idea why anyone would want his properties? Is it hopeless even trying to find out?"

Momma reached out and patted my hand. "Nothing is *ever* hopeless, my dear sweet child. I'll keep digging, don't you worry about that, and as soon as I learn anything important, I'll be more than happy to share it with you. Now, what's troubling you so?"

"Emma wants Donut Hearts," I said, the words tumbling out of me.

"What? What do you mean, she wants it? Suzanne, what's happened?"

"This morning, Emma and Sharon offered me a great deal of money for the shop," I said, explaining the provisions in Sharon's sister's will.

"It's odd, but it's probably perfectly legal," Momma said. "I could have my attorney research the matter for you if you'd like."

"No, that's not the part that's troubling me," I said. "When I told my book club what was going on, one of its members offered to buy the shop herself through her husband and his associates and let me stay on to run it. I don't know what to do."

Momma started to speak, and then she checked herself carefully. After a full minute, she asked, "What do *you* want, Suzanne?"

"I don't know," I admitted. "Part of me thinks I should take one of the offers. After all, how many am I going to get? Another part wants to keep Donut Hearts forever, but is that really that viable a business strategy? Emma and Sharon are offering me more than it's worth, that's for sure," I told her as I pulled out the wrinkled offer sheet and handed it to her.

She read it and then said, "As a matter of fact, it's a great deal more than it's worth. But that really doesn't matter, does it?"

"I've never heard you talk about money like that before," I told her. "You're *always* trying to make a profit on your business deals."

"But that's the point, isn't it? There are times where you have to listen to your heart and not your head. Let's break this down. That's what I often do: distill the deal to its essence. First let's consider your book club member's deal. How would you feel coming to work in someone else's shop, punching a time clock and just doing what you're told?"

When she put it that way, I didn't even have to think about it. "I wouldn't be too happy about it," I said.

"Then that's off the table. Call your friend now and tell her that if you're sure."

"Should I be so quick to dismiss her offer, though?" I asked. "It would take the pressure off me if I didn't have to worry about making much of a profit. Who knows? It might even be fun again under those conditions."

"As someone else's employee?" she asked me.

"No, that's true. Part of the joy of running Donut Hearts is knowing that I have complete autonomy in everything I do. If I fail, even if it's miserably, it's my gamble and my money, not someone else's."

"You have the same spirit I do, Suzanne," Momma said as she reached out and patted my hand. "When I fail, it is on my shoulders, but when I succeed, there's no other feeling in the world like it."

"When have *you* ever failed?" I asked her with a grin.

"More times than you would believe, but it's not the fact that I've gotten knocked down that I dwell on. It's the realization that I've always gotten back up, dusted myself off, and tried again. You have that same spirit. We weren't born to work for other people. Remember how miserable you were before you started Donut Hearts? You *detested* working for other people."

"Okay. That's all true."

"If you'd feel better talking it over with Jake first as well, I certainly won't be offended," Momma said quickly. "I was perhaps a bit rash telling you to make your decision instantly. It's your life, Suzanne, not mine."

"I appreciate all of your input, and there's no one whose advice I value more," I said. "If you're sure you're okay with it, I would like to talk it all over with Jake before I burn any bridges."

"A sound plan," Momma said as she stood. "I must be getting back to my husband. He'll be overjoyed with your kindness, as am I."

"I love you, Momma."

"I love you too, Suzanne. Remember, in the end, you need to go with your heart and not your head. If you do that, you *can't* make a mistake."

"I hope you're right," I told her. "Let me know if you hear anything else from your sources."

"I will. As for you, try to stay out of harm's way, would you? You are my only child, and my life would be unbearable without you in it."

It was one of my mother's most tender moments, and I leaned down and hugged her, clearly catching her by surprise, but not unhappily.

I watched her walk away, and then I headed back to my donut shop. It was still mine, at least for the moment, but I was going to take her advice. This decision needed to be what was best for me and no one else. It was okay, in this instance, to be selfish about it, and I was planning to do just that.

I hadn't been back at my front counter for more than five minutes when I was surprised to see Margaret and Gabby outside, heading toward the donut shop together. Since it was nearly closing time and neither woman was a frequent visitor to my shop, I doubted they were there for treats. That meant that it had something to do with Gary Shook's murder and how much progress I'd made so far in solving it.

It was not a conversation I was going to be all that happy about having, but short of bolting the door and running back into the kitchen to hide, I wasn't going to have all that much of a choice.

"Ladies, what can I get you today?" I asked them with the brightest smile I could manage.

"We're not here for donuts, Suzanne," Gabby said. "We want to know what progress you've made on the case so far."

I looked around at the three customers I had who were enjoying their donuts, and I shook my head. "Not here."

"We won't be…" Gabby started in on me, but I cut her off before she could protest any further.

"I said not here!" I snapped at her. It was a suicidal thing for most people to do to stomp on Gabby's sentence like that, but I couldn't let her intimidate me into admitting to the world that Grace and I were digging into Gary Shook's murder. I knew it was an open secret that we were investigating, but that didn't mean that I wanted all of April Springs to know it for a fact, especially the murderer. It wasn't that I thought anyone there at the time had killed the man, but I knew that if I acknowledged Gabby's claim, it would be all over town in an hour.

I honestly think Gabby was too surprised by my rebuff to even dispute it. Margaret, who had looked so determined coming into the shop, now looked at me and then her friend, with an air of uncertainty about her.

Holding up a finger, I walked from customer to customer explaining, "If I can't get you anything else, we're closing early today."

Only Mattie Jones protested. "I wanted more coffee," she said as she held out her mug.

"Tell you what. I'll make it a large one, and I'll throw in a free cinnamon donut if you get it to go. How does that sound?"

"Do I have to take the donut?" she asked.

"What's wrong? Not a fan of cinnamon?" I asked her.

"Not really. If the coffee offer is still good though, you've got yourself a deal."

I grabbed my biggest to-go cup, filled it with relatively fresh coffee, and then sent her on her way. I didn't bother flipping the sign to CLOSED, since I hadn't been serious.

I just didn't want any witnesses to the conversation I was about to have.

Once the three of us were alone, Gabby said, "Suzanne, I'm generally willing to give you some leeway in the way you behave given the stress you're under, but I won't be silenced like that again. Do I make myself clear?"

"I understand," I said, conceding the point now since it had absolutely no impact on my behavior. "I was just afraid that you were about to spoil any chance I had of solving Gary Shook's murder."

Gabby looked surprised by my claim. "How would I be able to do that?"

"Come on, Gabby, you know better than most folks the way this town likes to talk. If word gets out that Grace and I are investigating, people aren't going to be nearly as likely to trust us enough to speak with us candidly, and nobody wants that, do they?"

"Of course not," she said with a scoff in her voice. "I think you're overreacting, but I can abide by your desire for now."

"Gabby, let's not forget why we're here," Margaret said with a tremor in her voice. "Suzanne, have you made *any* progress?"

"These things take time," I told her. "We're doing the best we can, but it's still early. Did Jenny send you two over here to check up on me?"

"She doesn't even know that we're here," Margaret said, looking aghast at the very thought of it. "She's hiding in her apartment, hoping this is all going to blow over, but we all know that's not about to happen, is it?"

"No, murder doesn't just go away," I said.

Margaret nodded. "You need to work harder then." She reached into her oversized purse and pulled out a business envelope stuffed with something. As she put it on the counter and pushed it toward me, I could see that it was full of money, mostly ones, fives, and some tens from what I could see. If I had to guess, I would have said there was close to a thousand dollars there. "Take this."

"I told you that was a bad idea," Gabby scolded her friend.

"I don't care," Margaret replied.

I didn't make a move to touch the money. "What's going on, Margaret?"

"I just figured you might be a little more motivated if someone was *paying* you," she said. "Jenny needs your help, and if you don't figure out who killed that nasty man, the police are going to arrest my daughter."

"What makes you say that?"

"Let's be honest, Suzanne. It happened in the storeroom in her shop! Plus, it was no secret how much she disliked the man. It's the easiest thing in the world to arrest Jenny and be done with it, and the entire town knows it."

"Margaret, you're not giving our police chief enough credit," I told her.

"That young pup? He might be fine handing out traffic tickets and warnings to jaywalkers, but we're talking about murder here."

I touched the envelope lightly and pushed it back to her. "I'm not going to take your money."

She looked deflated. "Does that mean that you're giving up?"

"No, I'm still going to continue my investigation, but I'm not doing it for your cash."

"I told you that was how she would react," Gabby chided her friend softly. "Suzanne wouldn't take that money if she was stone broke. She's got principles." The last bit was the nicest compliment she had ever paid me, but I couldn't let my appreciation for it show, or I'd never get another from her.

Margaret reluctantly took the money and then looked me dead in the eye. "Suzanne, if you don't find the killer by this time tomorrow, then I'm going to confess."

"What? Don't say something like that you don't mean," Gabby told her friend.

"What makes you think I'm not serious?" she asked. "Do you think for one second that I'm going to stand idly by and watch my only child arrested for a crime she didn't commit? I gave her up once to my eternal regret, and I won't make that mistake again. Better that I should rot in jail for the rest of my life than allow her to spend one second of her life in jail."

"You can't do that, and what's more, you know it," I told her.

"What's stopping me?" Margaret asked defiantly.

"You didn't kill the man, for one thing," Gabby told her before I could answer her question.

"Chief Grant won't know that," Margaret insisted. "I can lie convincingly enough to get a jury to believe me, and if I'm in jail, then Jenny is free to live the rest of her life without this cloud hanging over her."

"You already tried that once, and the chief didn't believe you, remember?" I asked her. "What makes you think that you can convince him now?"

"Trust me, I can be *very* persuasive when the situation calls for it. He won't have any *choice* but to lock me up!"

I shook my head. "Even if it worked, which it won't, how do you think Jenny will feel believing that her birth mother is a cold-blooded killer?" I asked her.

Margaret wavered for a second before rebounding. "It's better she think that than be suspected of murder herself for the rest of her life," she said. "You've got twenty-four hours, Suzanne, and then I'm turning myself in, and I'll make it stick this time."

Margaret turned and walked out of the shop, and Gabby started after her. "You've got to talk her out of doing this, Gabby," I told her before she could leave. "It's not going to help anybody."

"I'll do what I can, but you need to find the real killer before she has a chance to ruin her life," Gabby answered.

"I'm doing everything in my power," I reminded her.

As Gabby walked out, she said, "Then do better."

I would if I could, but at the moment, I was nowhere near naming the killer yet, and now I had the added pressure of Margaret's repeated phony confession looming overhead.

If it was indeed phony.

Was it possible that *she* had actually killed Gary Shook herself? I couldn't discount it, but her offer to pay me to find the real murderer definitely gave me some doubt. Why would she do that if she'd been the one to skewer the landlord? I had no idea, but I wasn't comfortable enough to take her name off of our list yet.

It seemed like the deeper we dug, the darker the hole got.

Chapter 15

I WAS NEARLY READY to close the shop for the day, and maybe for the last time ever, when Cynthia Logan walked in just as I was about to flip the sign.

"I made it," she said, nearly out of breath from her sprint up the sidewalk. "I've been thinking about those donuts all morning, and I'd like to place a special order."

"This is your lucky day," I said. "I made some this morning after our conversation yesterday. As a matter of fact, I'll sell you the rest of the cinnamon cake donuts I have left for half price."

"Box them up! I'll gladly pay full retail," she said with a grin.

"I'm happy to give you a break on the price," I said as I started collecting the four dozen specialty donuts I had left.

"Thanks, but I'm already in enough hot water with my boss at the bank as it is. I'm a hair away from getting fired, and if he finds out I accepted a price break from a bank customer, I'd be out before the close of business today."

"I'm not exactly a big client," I admitted.

"Maybe not, but your mother certainly is," Cynthia said.

"While I've got you here, have you thought any more about my question about Gary Shook's properties? What's going to happen to them now that he's dead?"

Since we were alone in the shop, it felt as though she was in more of a mood to share information with me than she had been earlier. "The truth is that he was in arrears on his mortgage payments, so we're going to take the property back and sell it ourselves to try to cover our losses," she explained.

"What about the buyer who wanted it originally?" I asked her.

Her smile dimmed. "As I said before, I'm not at liberty to discuss that."

"How about if we do it as a hypothetical?" I asked her.

Cynthia seemed to consider that as a possibility. "I might be able to do that. Let's say that the property was about to be in default anyway and the owner suddenly died. The bank could always expedite the foreclosure if it had someone interested in picking the property up quickly without any conditions attached to it, but they'd have to know the right people to make that happen."

"Are you one of those right people?" I asked her.

"I'm afraid that kind of decision is well above my pay grade. My boss would have to approve that himself."

"Is that what's going on with the strip mall?" I asked her pointblank.

She looked frustrated by the constraints placed on her. "Suzanne, I'd tell you if I could, but I'm doing my best to stay out of it. As things stand, I'm in trouble enough as it is. I'm half expecting to lose my job due to overextending that loan as long as I did, so if anything's going on with that property right now, I'm not a part of it." She handed me the money and gleefully took the donuts from me. "I can't believe how lucky I feel getting these."

"I hope you enjoy them," I said with the best smile I could muster. Was I barking up the wrong tree thinking that Gary Shook's murder had something to do with him trying to sell his real estate? Had it all just been a simple case of an angry renter seizing the opportunity to snuff him out once and for all? Or could it have been that he'd chosen the wrong woman to intimidate, and she'd turned him down in the most emphatic way possible? I wasn't sure, and I needed to find out, and soon.

The clock was ticking, and I felt as though I was running out of time on just about every front I was fighting at the moment.

I was finally ready to close Donut Hearts, so I called out to Emma, "That's a wrap."

She tore out of the kitchen as though it were on fire. "Do you need me to help you close? I just got a text from Mom. She needs me down at the bank."

"No, feel free to go. Have a good afternoon and evening," I told her.

"You, too," Emma said quickly as she bolted out the door.

As she did, she nearly knocked Grace over, who was trying to come in at the same time.

"Hi, Emma. Bye, Emma," Grace said as my assistant nearly ran to her car. "Where's the fire?" she asked me.

"She couldn't wait to get out of here, and I don't blame her one bit. We had ourselves a day," I said as I locked the door behind her. "Have a seat, and I'll tell you all about it."

"You haven't been digging into Gary Shook's murder without me, have you?"

"You know the way this place works. There are times when I can't keep my suspects away," I told her.

"So, what did you find out?" Grace asked as she poured herself a cup of coffee and grabbed a cruller from the rack. When she saw that I was watching her, she grinned. "You don't mind, do you?"

"Not at all. Please help yourself," I said with a smile.

"Don't mind if I do," she answered. "I'll pitch in as soon as I finish this."

"Hang on. Let me see how bad the kitchen looks first." I went in back and was pleasantly surprised to see that things were in perfect order there, all the dishes washed and put away. I still had some racks to wash and I needed to sweep the front after cleaning the tables, but it wouldn't be too daunting without Emma helping me.

I came back to find Grace grabbing another donut. "It's just an old-fashioned," she said. "It hardly counts as calories at all."

"Keep telling yourself that," I said with a smile.

"Yeah, maybe you're right," she said as she put it in a bag. "I'll save this for later. After all, I don't want to ruin my appetite for lunch."

"We can't have that," I said as I started the register running its report as I counted out the money in the till. Grace knew better than to talk to me while I was totaling my cash. Once I had my physical totals, it was just a matter of waiting on the register to finish running.

Grace had finished her snack by then and asked me, "What can I do?"

"You can wipe down the tables while I box the rest of the donuts and wash the racks," I said.

"I can do that."

We had the place clean in no time, and the report was finally finished running. My totals were spot on, which was a relief, as I was in no mood to sort through it all, reconciling my balances for the day. I made out the deposit slip, and then I looked around the place lovingly.

Grace just stood there in silence, clearly picking up on my somber mood. When I was ready to go, I turned to her and asked, "Shall we?"

"We shall," she said. "Suzanne, what's going on? Something's really eating at you, isn't it?"

"Could we just not talk about it for a few minutes?" I asked her. "I need a little time."

"Take all you need," she said. "Just remember, I'm here for you."

I reached out and squeezed her hand. "I know, and I appreciate it." We walked out to my Jeep, and I added, "Let's drop this by the bank, and then we can go get a bite to eat before we get started, if you're still hungry, that is."

"Try me," she said with a grin.

We were on our way to the bank when I said, "Oh, by the way, Margaret tried to pay us to investigate Gary Shook's murder."

"How much did we get?" she asked happily.

"I didn't take it," I told her sternly.

"I know that, you nit. I was joking. I wonder what that was all about?"

"She's obviously desperate to save Jenny. Gabby came with her to the donut shop earlier, and she tried to talk Margaret out of it, but she wouldn't listen to her."

"She's a brave woman to go against Gabby Williams," she said with obvious respect.

"I have a feeling that Margaret feels as though desperate times call for desperate measures. When paying us didn't work, she threatened to confess to the murder again in twenty-four hours if we haven't solved it by then."

Grace looked at me oddly. "She's tried that already, and Stephen didn't buy it." Grace hesitated a moment before asking, "You don't think she actually *did* it, do you?"

"No, not really, but she is clearly willing to do whatever it takes to keep Jenny out of jail," I explained as I pulled up in front of the bank.

"Then that means that she thinks there's a chance that *Jenny* did it," Grace said.

"I think so. She claims Chief Grant is going to use her daughter as a scapegoat." Grace was about to interrupt when I continued, "I told her that she was being ridiculous, but there was no talking to her." I grabbed the deposit bag. "I want to take this inside today."

"Okay," she said as she grabbed the leftover donuts, greatly diminished by the last-second sale of the triple-cinnamon specials. "I'll catch up on some emails while you do, unless you need me with you in there."

I hadn't told her about Cynthia coming by the shop or anything else that I'd learned yet. There would be time for that after I finished my banking, but I wanted to see how Cynthia reacted to my sudden presence. I wasn't sure why, but I felt as though she was on edge about something, as though she wanted to tell me more about Gary's situation but didn't feel comfortable disclosing too much. I had to respect that, especially since she'd said that her job was on the line. Maybe if I got a word with her on familiar territory, she'd feel more willing to share more information with me. Then again, maybe not, but it was worth a shot, and I was starting to feel as though this investigation was stalling from a lack of new information. It was time to shake the trees a bit and see what might fall out.

I never got the chance to speak with her, though. Cynthia was in the branch manager's office, and from the look of things, it wasn't going well for her. His back was to me, but Cynthia was facing me, and when she spotted me, I could see a pained expression on her face.

I wasn't going to be getting anything more out of her today; that much was pretty clear.

I made my deposit and rejoined Grace, who looked up and grinned. "Wow, that was fast."

"Some days it's like that," I said. "What are you smiling about?"

"I just found out that I won the sales contest. Well, second place, anyway. Woohoo!"

"That's excellent. What are you going to do with the money?"

"Spend it on something decadent, no doubt," she said.

"And the day off?" I asked.

"I'm not sure. Maybe I'll have myself a spa day. Why don't you take a day off and go with me?"

"I just might take you up on that." I turned the ignition on and said, "I'm ready to talk now. Let's drive around town so nobody interrupts us. Which do you want to hear about first, the personal stuff or the investigation?"

"Always the personal," she said eagerly. "It hurts that you even have to ask."

"I know, but I wanted to give you the choice. Emma and Sharon want to buy Donut Hearts outright, and if I don't sell it to them, Jennifer from my book club is putting a deal together to buy the shop and have me stay on as the manager." It felt weird having those words come out of my mouth.

To Grace's credit, she didn't react instantly. Instead, she took a deep breath and then finally said, "That's a lot to process."

"Think how I feel," I said.

"How can Emma and Sharon afford to buy Donut Hearts?" she asked me.

"They got an inheritance they have to use to buy a business, and the one they seem to want is mine." I told her what the offer was, and I saw her eyes widen.

After a good ten seconds, I asked her, "Don't you have anything to say?"

"Suzanne, do you *need* money right now?"

"No, I'm good," I answered.

"Then the next question is do you *want* to sell Donut Hearts?" Her question was what I'd been asking myself since early that morning.

"There are some real advantages to doing it now," I said. "Jake and I would be set for a long time, I wouldn't have to deal with the daily headaches of running a business that's always on the brink of bankruptcy, and we could do some traveling when Jake's not working."

"When he is, though, what are you going to do with your life? You aren't thinking about working with him on a full-time basis, are you?" Grace asked me with obvious concern in her voice.

"No, that didn't go particularly well for either one of us last time," I admitted. "We make a good team, but I have a feeling that Jake is better off without me when he's on a consulting job."

"That's fair. After all, he wouldn't last long working with you at the donut shop, either," Grace reminded me.

"There's no doubt about that. I'm afraid if I turn both offers down, I'll never get another one," I told her. "What do you think I should do?"

"Oh, no, I'm not about to answer that."

I looked at her and frowned. "Seriously? You have opinions about my clothes, my hair, even what I have for breakfast, but *this* you don't have a position on one way or the other?"

"I didn't say that," she answered calmly. "I've absolutely got an opinion. I'm just not going to tell you what it is."

"May I ask why not?" I queried.

"Sure, you can ask."

When she didn't say anything, I prodded her. "I'm asking."

"What *I* think doesn't matter. It's what *you* think that counts. Have you spoken with Jake about it yet?"

"No, I was going to wait until this evening," I admitted.

"Well, don't count on him trying to convince you that one option is better than the other one for you. Unless I wildly miss my guess, he's too smart for that."

"So *nobody's* going to help me?" I asked her, feeling frustrated by the lack of guidance I was getting from my mother and my best friend. To top it off, if Grace was right, Jake would be no better. It appeared that I was going to have to figure this out for myself.

"You might not realize it, but that's exactly what we're all doing," Grace said. "It all boils down to one thing; what do *you* want to do?"

"At the moment? I want to get a bite to eat, work on Gary Shook's murder investigation, and forget all about Donut Hearts for a few hours. Do you think that's even possible?"

"I'm not sure, but I'll do my best to help you find out. Did you learn anything else about the case today?"

I brought her up to speed on my thoughts and observations, finishing up with Cynthia's apparent rebuke at the bank a few minutes earlier.

Grace said, "We probably can't count on her for any more information about the property, but I'm sure that your mother will come through for us. She always does."

"Let's hope so. That leaves us with our suspect list then," I said. "We've got Jenny, Margaret, Lawrence, and Cheryl."

"Cynthia, too," Grace reminded me. "She could be tied up in this somehow, too."

"I suppose so," I said. "In that case, we should keep our eyes and ears open for other suspects. Gary Shook made a great many waves around here, didn't he? Then again, I can't imagine murder being performed so casually and carelessly. It obviously wasn't well planned out."

"How can you say that?" Grace asked me as I pulled up in front of The Boxcar Grill, nearly exactly where we'd started from earlier. I didn't care; driving around had been an important way to buy us some time alone to talk.

"My gut is telling me that whoever followed Gary Shook into the For The Birds storeroom didn't have murder on their mind at the time. Why else would they use something they found in the shop itself? I believe that whoever stabbed Gary did so rashly, probably in the heat of the moment."

"Maybe so, but he's still just as dead as if they'd planned it," Grace said. "So, do we think the motive was because of the imminent evictions or something sleazy Gary tried to do?"

"It could have been both," I said, remembering the scene with Molly that my stepfather had overheard being recounted.

"True enough. Margaret and Cynthia were the only ones not directly involved with the sudden rent increases, which gives them a *little* less motive than the others," Grace answered.

"And I doubt that Gary had any amorous inclinations toward Lawrence based on what we've learned of the murder victim and his history with women."

"We certainly can't rule it out, but it's doubtful based on his behavior," Grace agreed.

"So that leaves us with Jenny, Molly, and Cheryl as our prime suspects," I said.

"With Margaret, Cynthia, and Lawrence in our secondary group," she added.

"That gives us six suspects, and any one of them could have done it. Not only that, but there's a chance that someone not even on our radar did it," I said a bit glumly.

"Don't think that way," Grace said. "If we go down that particular rabbit hole, there's no getting out of it. Let's just focus on the six we have and see where that leads us."

"Agreed," I said. "But let's do it *after* we eat lunch. If you're not hungry, you can just sit there and keep me company while I eat."

Grace laughed. "Yeah, like that's going to happen. It was one donut, Suzanne."

"It was a cruller, and a big one at that," I countered.

"Whatever. Come on. Let's eat."

"I'm right behind you," I said with a grin. I knew that I had some big decisions to make, but for the moment, it felt good being able to focus on something else.

Chapter 16

"LADIES, I HOPE YOU'RE both hungry," Trish said as we walked into the Boxcar.

"We usually are," I told her. "What's up?"

"Hilda's trying out a new recipe, and she's asked me to single out only the most discerning of palates to taste it," the diner owner replied.

"And you want us?" Grace asked her with a grin.

"Why not? You both have good taste, right?"

"I like to think I have a certain flair," Grace said, "and Suzanne does the best she can with her limited abilities." I was glad she laughed as she said the last bit.

"That's certainly true. There are days I can't seem to remember whether my socks go on first or my shoes," I replied.

"And yet we love you despite all of that," Trish said happily. "Have a seat."

"May we at least ask what we'll be eating?" I asked her.

"No, I don't want to ruin the surprise," Trish answered.

Five minutes later, she brought out two large bowls and a plate with crusty bread on it. "What's this?" I asked as she put it down in front of me. "Stew?"

"Lower your voice," Trish said. "Trust me, you don't want to offend Hilda."

"It looks great," I said loudly, and Grace smiled and nodded as well.

I wasn't expecting much as I dipped my spoon into the bowl, but after I took my first taste, my pleasure was real enough. "This is amazing. What is it?"

"She won't tell me the exact ingredients, but I love it, too. What do you say? Should we put it on the menu? It's going to be a bit pricey for our crowd, but I think it deserves a spot."

"I agree. It's worth whatever it's going to cost," I said diving into it again. There were spices lying just below the surface that set my taste buds dancing, and the more I ate of it, the more I wanted.

"Grace? What do you think?" Trish asked.

"I'm not sure. I may have to have a few more bowls before I can give you a definitive answer," she replied with a broad smile.

I saw Grace give two thumbs up in the direction of the kitchen and realized that Hilda had been watching us from the start. "Well done," I told her happily, and I saw her grin as she ducked back into her domain.

"Have you been by Two Cows and a Moose lately?" Trish asked us as we were settling up our bill. She hadn't wanted to charge us, but there was no way that Grace and I were going to let her serve us that amazing food without paying for it.

"Not for a while," I admitted. "What's up?"

"Go by as soon as you get the chance. You won't be sorry," she said as she gave us our change.

Once we were outside, I asked Grace, "What do you think? Can we spare a minute to check Emily's business out?"

"After that buildup, I don't see how we can't," she said.

"That is hilarious," I said the moment I spotted Cow, Spots, and Moose on their shelf in their place of honor. My friend Emily had loved those stuffed animals since she'd been a kid, and they were prominently displayed above the register, which was only fitting, since her shop had been named after them. She often outfitted them to match the season, and this was no exception. We might have been in the waning moments of summer, but you'd never know it from their attire. The two cows and the moose were dressed in Hawaiian shirts, sported sunglasses, and wore leis around their necks, and they even had strips of white tape across their snouts that mimicked sunscreen. Most of those accessories had been used before in different combinations, but this time she'd added something completely different to the mix. Each stuffed animal now had a decorated surfboard propped up behind them, appropriately sized of course.

"Aren't they adorable?" Emily asked as she spotted us admiring them.

"They are fantastic! Where did you find those surfboards?" I asked her.

"Max made them himself," she said. "He's really embraced my friends."

Max had been a terrible husband to me, but he'd changed since then, and now he was perfect for Emily. I might have resented it if it weren't for the fact that I'd found Jake, but I was honestly happy for them.

"Why wouldn't he?" Grace asked. "They're the best."

"Don't think they don't realize exactly how cool they look, either," Emily said softly. Why was she whispering? Was it because she didn't want them to overhear her praise? Sometimes when I talked to her about her stuffed animals, I wasn't completely sure that she knew they weren't really alive.

"It's hard to dispute," I said. "How's business?"

"We're keeping our head above water," she said. "You?"

"About the same," I replied.

"Well, keep swinging. One of these days we'll all be rich and famous."

"Rich I could stand; famous not so much," I told her.

Once we were back outside, Grace asked, "Didn't Gary Shook live near here?"

"I have no idea," I admitted. "How could you possibly know that?"

Grace grinned. "I looked his address up last night. Why don't we swing by his place and see if there's anything there we might be able to see?"

"How do you propose we get inside?" I asked her. "We've tried breaking and entering before, and it's never worked out for us."

"Relax, Suzanne. I'm not suggesting we do anything illegal. If the door's locked, then we'll do what everyone else does."

"What's that?"

"We'll peek through the window," she said happily.

I realized there was no reason to fight her on it. I wouldn't mind seeing his place myself. Who knew? If we got lucky, maybe we'd be able to see something that would help us figure out who had killed the man. It wasn't that likely, but it was at least worth a shot.

"It's locked," Grace said as she rattled the front doorknob.

"Are you surprised that it is?" I asked her. "I can't see a thing through this window. The blind is pulled all the way down."

"*Nearly* all the way, you mean," Grace said as she squatted down and looked inside. "Suzanne, check it out."

I got down too, wondering how it would look if anyone spotted us there, but I didn't care anymore once I got a glimpse inside his apartment.

It had been completely and thoroughly trashed, at least what we could see of it. Kitchen cupboards had been thrown open and emptied, an end table in the living room was on its side, and a thick sheaf of papers littered the floor. "That's not from a police search," I said.

"I agree," she said as she pulled out her cell phone. "I'm calling Stephen."

"Isn't he going to want to know what we were doing here?" I asked her before she could complete the call.

"He knows we're snooping, Suzanne," Grace said, "but he needs to hear about this. Do you agree?"

"I do," I said. After all, the chief of police needed to know what was going on in his own town, and we had no right to keep any pertinent information from him.

"Thanks for calling me," Chief Grant said after he got out of his cruiser and approached us.

"We couldn't get in," Grace said, "but it's clear enough that *someone* has."

He squatted down and looked inside. "What a mess."

"I take it your people didn't do that?" I asked him.

"If they did, I'd fire them on the spot. The landlord is meeting me here in a few minutes. Isn't there someplace else you two need to be?"

"We could always hang around and help you investigate," I said with a shrug.

"I appreciate the offer, but I've got it covered. I'll talk to you both later." The dismissal was clear and final.

"We'll be around," I said.

I saw a quick exchange of glances between Grace and her fiancé, and I looked away. They deserved at least that much privacy.

"I don't get it. What was someone looking for?" Grace asked me as we drove to the strip mall where the businesses and, more importantly, the people we needed to see, were located.

"I have no idea," I said, "but I'm guessing it was written down on something."

"There were an awful lot of papers on the floor, weren't there?"

I agreed. "That's something, anyway."

"Sure. All we have to do is look at every piece of paper we can find that Gary Shook may have been hiding and figure out what was important enough for someone to break into his apartment to try to find. Piece of cake."

"For a pair of crack investigators like us? Simple as simple could be," I said with a smile. "So, who do we tackle first? I'm guessing we need to speak with each of the tenants that are here."

"Do you think some of them will be gone already?" I asked Grace as I got closer. "Surely Jenny and Cheryl both have loose ends to wrap up, even if they are leaving."

"Let's hope so," she said.

At least there were cars parked in front of all of the shops. I decided to park in front of For The Birds and tackle Jenny first. With any luck, Margaret would be helping her close things out, so we could kill two birds with one stone, no matter how inappropriate that saying seemed at the moment.

Grace headed for the front door when I noticed someone watching us from inside the nail salon. The only problem was that it wasn't Cheryl.

It was Lawrence.

What was he doing there, and what was he looking for?

"Grace, let's check that place out first," I said as I pointed to the salon. Lawrence chose that moment to duck back out of sight, but she'd seen him too.

"What is up with that?" she asked me.

"I don't know, so let's find out."

I knocked on the door for a good minute before Cheryl came out. Her hair was mussed and she'd mis-buttoned her top. That was bad enough, but her face was flushed as she answered the door. "Sorry, I didn't hear you. I was in back."

I stepped inside and called out, "We saw you before, Lawrence. You might as well come out."

There was no response, and Cheryl protested, "I'm here by myself."

"He didn't have time to get out the back way," Grace answered. "Don't make us come back there and get you!" She sounded like a stern schoolteacher. I was afraid that he might have already escaped when I heard movement, and clearly Cheryl heard it, too.

"It's okay. You can come out."

Lawrence joined us, and I noticed a smudge of lipstick on his collar. Too much added up to mean anything else.

"How long have you two been an item?" I asked them, and an instant later Cheryl burst into tears.

Smooth, Suzanne, really smooth.

Lawrence went to console her, and the way she melted into his arms made it apparent that they were closer than just co-tenants in the strip mall. "You can't tell anyone, Suzanne. Grace, you can't either."

"What exactly don't you want us to say?" I asked her.

"We both lied to you before," Cheryl told us.

"You don't have to do this," Lawrence said after they'd split up.

"I'm tired of keeping it a secret," she said firmly. Cheryl turned to us and said, "I don't know if you even know this, but I've been married to a very bad man for much too long. He's in jail right now, but he's getting out next week. I haven't loved him for years, but I thought I was going to be doomed to be in his life forever, and then Lawrence came along."

"If he's in jail, why are you sneaking around?" I asked them.

"He's had some of his friends keeping an eye on me," she said hesitantly. "That's why I lied to you about my alibi."

"I lied, too," Lawrence said, "but it was in the name of love. I couldn't tell you where I really was. I was over here with Cheryl."

"Part of what I told you was true. I drove around until I lost the guy tailing me, and then I came straight here," she admitted. "Benny's been suspicious of me and Lawrence for a while now, and I knew it was stupid to see him again, but I couldn't help myself."

"What about you taking the job at the nail salon in Union Square?" Grace asked. "You're not exactly leaving the area."

"It was all just a smoke screen," Lawrence said. "Cheryl's closing this place up, and I'm selling my shop to one of my customers. We're running away together where Benny will never be able to find us."

"You could always try to get a divorce," I suggested. A life on the run was no life at all, at least as far as I was concerned.

"I'm doing that," she said. "It will be final tomorrow, and we're getting married and moving away forever."

I couldn't imagine uprooting myself from everything and everyone I knew, but there was one circumstance in which I would do it in a heartbeat without looking back, and that was if it was for Jake.

"We didn't have anything to do with Gary Shook's death," Lawrence said. "How could we? We were together when it must have happened, at least for the short time I was gone from my shop. We were here together, talking to her lawyer about finalizing the divorce. Call Henry Carter in Hudson. He'll vouch for us."

"The two of us were going over the paperwork before Lawrence got here for hours, so he's my alibi, too," Cheryl said. "We don't want to be here, Suzanne. We can't be here," she said.

I looked at Grace. "What do you think?"

"I believe them," she said. "It's too easy to check on."

"Why *wouldn't* you believe us?" Lawrence asked. "It's the truth."

"They just need to be sure, honey," Cheryl told him. At first glance, they made an odd couple, but who was I to say who belonged together and who didn't? Max and I had looked good on paper, but we'd been a disaster married to each other, while Jake and I were a stretch for many reasons, but there was no doubt in my mind or my heart that we belonged together.

"Okay, let's say for now that we believe you," I said. "What can we do to help?"

Grace looked at me and grinned. "Cupid's warriors, at your service."

"We're afraid we're going to be followed when we leave," Lawrence said. "Can you do anything to help us?"

"That depends. Cheryl, is your car out front?"

"It's parked in its usual spot," she said. "Why?"

I ignored her question. "Lawrence, do they know what kind of car you drive?"

"I wouldn't think so," he said.

"Here's what we're going to do then. Give me your keys and tell me what you're driving, Lawrence. I'll pull around to the back door, and you can both leave from there. They won't suspect me if I'm getting in-to your car even if they know what you're driving."

"That's a good idea, but *I* need to be the one driving it," Grace said.

"Why is that?"

"If they're out there, they saw you driving the Jeep when we got here. They'll never believe that you have two cars here, Suzanne, but they don't have any idea that Lawrence's car isn't mine."

"That's a fair point," I said. "Are you sure about taking the risk?"

"There's no risk in my mind," Grace said. "Besides, it sounds like fun."

"It sounds dangerous to me," Lawrence said. "I can't let you take that chance for us."

"It's the only way," Cheryl said pleadingly. "Please?"

He nodded after a moment as he handed Grace his keys. "If anyone tries to stop you or follow you, don't come back here," he instructed her.

"Don't worry about me. I've been cloaking and daggering for years," she said with a smile.

I stopped Grace at the door. "Be careful."

"You bet," she replied.

I started to watch out the window, and then I decided that the less attention I paid to what Grace was doing, the better. That didn't mean that I couldn't cause a distraction to help her, though. Without saying a word, I followed her and went straight to my Jeep. After pretending that it wouldn't start, I lifted the hood as Grace started Lawrence's car and drove away. I saw two men sitting in a parked car nearby watching me, but the moment they saw me walking toward them as I asked them loudly for help, they drove off in the opposite direction.

Shrugging for show, I closed the hood and walked back inside.

"That was brilliant," Cheryl said with a smile.

"I figured it couldn't hurt," I answered.

"She's here," Lawrence called out from the back, and Cheryl and I joined them. Grace handed him the keys as she winked at me. "Good acting, Suzanne. Max would be proud."

"I kind of doubt that, but thanks anyway," I said. "Are you two going to be okay?" I asked as I turned to them.

"We will now," Cheryl said as she hugged us both. Lawrence gave us a goofy grin and a wave as he opened her car door, and at the last second, I realized something.

"How do we close up your shop, Cheryl?"

She flung the keys to me and smiled. "Lock up the place, and feel free to use my car if you need it. I'll let you know when I'm ready for it again."

After they were gone, Grace asked, "Well, what do you think about that?"

"I wouldn't have believed it before, but seeing them together, I think they make a good match. Grace, we didn't just help a killer escape, did we? Maybe even two?"

"No, I believe them," she said, "but let's call that attorney and be sure, just in case."

We did, and the lawyer told us that he'd just heard from his client. She'd given him permission to talk to us, and their stories were verified that easily.

We'd suddenly gone from six people to worry about down to four, which was an improvement for sure, but we still had a long way to go before we found the killer. Otherwise, Margaret was going to confess and throw everything into turmoil.

I just hoped we could wrap the case up before I had to meet the *other* deadline that was looming over me.

Chapter 17

"WHAT'S GOING ON, JENNY?" I asked her the second we walked into the nearly empty storefront where For The Birds was just the day before.

"Hey, Suzanne," she said as she dabbed at her eyes. It was clear that she'd been crying when we'd walked in, but she was trying to act as though nothing had happened. "Hi, Grace."

"Why are you crying?" I asked her. "Are you upset about Lawrence and Cheryl?" I was taking a wild guess, but what else could have made her so sad? I couldn't imagine it being Gary Shook's murder suddenly hitting her so hard.

"What about them?" she asked me curiously.

"It's supposed to be a secret, but they're running away together," Grace told her.

"Finally, some good news," Jenny said as she dabbed at her cheeks. "I knew that they'd been seeing each other, but I wasn't sure that anyone else did. I can't believe they told you."

"Are you kidding?" Grace asked. "We helped them get away."

"I can't believe they really pulled the trigger," she said. "Good for them."

"So you're not upset about Lawrence?" I asked.

"We were nothing more than friends," she told me. "Ever since I've known him, he's had a huge crush on Cheryl. I knew she liked him too, but given her... er, circumstances, I wasn't sure it was going to work out for them."

"So, if you're not upset about that, then why exactly were you crying when we walked in?" Grace pressed her.

"I wasn't crying," she protested as she tried to avoid eye contact with us.

"Jenny, if we haven't proven to you that we're friends by now after helping you with your close-out sale and everything else we've done since, then I don't even know why we're bothering to try to solve Gary Shook's murder for you," I said bluntly. The words were harsh, but she wasn't about to get away with lying to us, not after what we'd been trying to do on her behalf. I didn't feel as though I had any choice; I had to do *something* to shock her into telling us the truth once and for all. "Come on, Grace. Let's go. It's over."

I was proud of my sidekick for not even hesitating. As I walked toward the door, Grace was right beside me, though I hadn't told her that I was going to try to force Jenny into talking to us.

"Wait!" Jenny nearly shouted. "You can't leave me here alone!"

"Then tell us the truth," I told her. "What's got you so upset?"

"It's my mother," she uttered, the words clearly breaking her heart.

"What about her?" I asked.

"I think she might have killed Gary Shook, and it's all my fault."

Chapter 18

"WHAT ARE YOU TALKING about?" I asked her. "Did she *say* something to you?"

"No, but I made a huge mistake, and she was trying to fix it for me."

"We're going to need more than that," Grace said softly. "What did you tell her?"

"The mistake I made was telling her how much it was going to kill me having to shut down For The Birds," she told us. "A few days ago, I told her that I wished I didn't have to go through with shutting my business down, but Gary Shook wasn't going to change his mind about jacking up my rent, so there was no way I could keep going. She told me not to worry about it, that she'd make sure it wouldn't happen. I explained to her that it was already a done deal and that we were going to sell all of my stock. Margaret assured me that we could always resupply even if we went through with the sale. I kept protesting that it was impossible, and she kept saying that nothing was impossible or out of the question when it came to her baby girl. She killed him for me. I just know it."

"Well, I don't," I said. "*You* might think that it's possible, but without proof, you're just guessing just like everyone else in town. Don't you think she at least *deserves* your benefit of the doubt?" I asked her. "Wouldn't you do that for a complete stranger?"

"Of course I would," she said. "It's just that she's tried so hard to make it up to me for giving me up for adoption all those years ago."

"That may be true, but it doesn't make her a killer," I said.

"You're right," she said, her words spoken barely above a whisper.

"This isn't going to help matters, but there's something you need to know," I said.

"Suzanne, don't," Grace warned me, but I couldn't have Jenny hearing it from her own birth mother if we failed to name the killer by the next day.

"I don't have much choice," I said.

Grace seemed to mull it over for a few seconds before she nodded. "You're right. Go ahead and tell her."

"Tell me what?" Jenny asked.

"Margaret tried to pay us to find Gary Shook's killer," I told her, which was the softer news I had to share with her about the woman.

"She what?" Jenny asked hesitantly.

"I'm guessing it was her life's savings, too," I said.

"But if she killed Gary Shook, why would she pay you to find his killer?" she asked me.

"Or why would you ask us to do the same thing the day before?" I added. "It doesn't make a lot of sense, does it?"

Jenny seemed to chew on that for a moment. "Hang on a second. Grace, you didn't want Suzanne to tell me something, but this makes Margaret look innocent. There's more, isn't there?"

I couldn't lie to her. Jenny would see right through it. "When I told her that she couldn't pay us to do something we were already doing for free, she gave us a deadline. This doesn't mean that it's true, okay? She's just at her wit's end trying to protect you."

"What is it, Suzanne?"

I took a deep breath, and then I told her. "She said that if we didn't find the killer by tomorrow, she was going to confess and make it stick this time, whether she did it or not."

"Why would she do that?" Jenny asked, clearly troubled by the implications of the action. "Does she honestly think that *I* did it?" she pondered aloud in shocked horror.

"No, I'm sure it's not that at all," I was quick to say. "She's afraid that if the chief of police doesn't find the real killer soon, he's going to focus on you, and Margaret is worried that it will ruin your life even if it isn't true."

"I tried to tell her that Stephen Grant is a better man than that, and a much more capable chief of police than she's giving him credit for, but she's panicking, plain and simple," Grace answered.

"What am I going to do?" Jenny asked, her eyes tearing up just as the front door opened.

Molly Davis burst in, took in the scene, and immediately misread it. "What are you two doing browbeating Jenny like this? Doesn't she have enough problems without having her *friends* turn on her in her time of need?"

"It's okay," Jenny said. "They're just trying to help."

"By upsetting you like this?" Molly asked. "Suzanne, Grace, you both need to leave."

"We'll go when Jenny tells us to," I said firmly. "Right, Grace?"

"Right," she answered.

Molly stared at Jenny for a second. "Well? Do they go, or do I?"

"Molly, *nobody* has to leave. They're on my side," Jenny said as she started to cry again.

"If anyone's upsetting her, it's you," Grace said coolly.

"Then *I'll* go," Molly replied as she stormed off.

"What's her problem?" Grace asked us.

"She's worried about me, that's all," Jenny said. "I need to go after her and make sure she's all right."

"She'll be fine," I said. "Right now, we need to focus on you."

Jenny shook her head. "I know you two are my friends, but so is Molly. I have to go."

With that, she left us in her shop, or what remained of it. Honestly, there was nothing left there worth bothering with. So why had she been there in the first place? Was it a pang of what she was leaving behind, or was she returning to the scene of the crime? I had been fairly certain that Jenny was innocent before, but I was beginning to have my doubts now.

"We might as well go, too," I told Grace when I realized that they weren't coming back.

"Is it just me, or was that weird? I've known Jenny for years, but the way she's acting right now makes me wonder if I ever really knew her at all." She hesitated a moment before adding, "Suzanne, I'm not so sure that she didn't do it."

"I'm not, either," I admitted. "And what was with Molly? She pretty much attacked us from the second she came into the shop, and when Jenny wouldn't choose her over us, she stormed off."

"Frankly, I don't think either one of them has done anything lately to make me think they're innocent," Grace said. "Suzanne, is there a chance they were in on it together?"

"What do you mean?" I asked her.

"What if one of them killed Gary and the other one witnessed it, or even stood guard as it was happening? That might explain this sudden bond between them. It's almost as though Molly didn't trust Jenny to be alone with us and that Jenny didn't really want us there, either."

"I have no idea if you're right or not, but we need to dig into both of them more," I said as my cell phone rang.

It was my mother. "Hey, Momma. What's up? Have you made any progress finding out about Gary Shook's real estate dealings?"

"No, both of my main sources won't be back in town until tomorrow morning. Must I have a reason to call my daughter?"

"You don't *have* to have one, but you generally do," I said.

"Phillip and I were wondering if you'd like to have dinner with us tonight," she said.

"Thanks, but I thought I'd probably just grab something to eat with Grace."

"Sorry, but I can't," Grace interrupted. "I've got a date with Stephen in ten minutes. I could always cancel if you wanted me to."

"Don't you dare," I said as I put my hand over the phone. "Good news, Momma, I'm suddenly free."

"Excellent. Why don't you come by as soon as you can? It will give us a chance to chat about something that's been on my mind lately."

That certainly sounded mysterious enough. "Care to give me a hint what it's about?" I asked her cagily.

"When we see you will be soon enough," she said. "As I say, come over any time."

"I'll see you soon then," I told her.

"What was that all about?" Grace asked me.

"I have no idea. I'm sorry, I didn't realize you had a date," I told her.

"That's because I just found out about it myself. Stephen has a little free time, and I wasn't about to say no. I hope you don't mind."

I smiled at my best friend. "Feel free to stand me up anytime," I said with a grin. "At least if it's for your fiancé."

"Duly noted," she said. "Do you feel good leaving things where they are at the moment?"

"I'm not sure we have much choice," I said. "At least Emma and Sharon are running Donut Hearts tomorrow, so I'm free to investigate with you all day if you can find the time."

"For you, I'll even take that day off I just won," she said. As we drove back to our respective homes, Grace asked, "What are you going to do about Donut Hearts?"

"Honestly? I don't have a clue."

"Trust your heart, Suzanne," she repeated as she got out of the Jeep and walked toward her home. "It will never let you down."

"Unlike my head, right?" I asked her with a grin.

"Well, you *do* still have to work out that shoe/sock problem, so yeah, if I were you, I'd probably go with my gut." She paused and then said, "There's no right or wrong answer. The only correct thing to do is what you want."

"And what if I don't know what that is?" I asked her.

"Then flip a coin," she said with a grin.

"Thanks. You are so helpful," I answered sarcastically.

"Hey, all you have to do is ask, and I'm right here," she replied with a smile.

I turned around and headed over to Momma's house, wondering what was suddenly so important. I wasn't sure I was going to be happy with the subject matter, but I was pretty sure I was going to enjoy the meal, and honestly, given that, it was a trade-off I'd normally make ten times out of ten.

At least the pair of them waited until after dinner to start in on me. As Momma and I were clearing the dishes after dining on one of her wonderful pot roasts, she said, "I've been giving your conundrum some thought, Suzanne, and I believe I may have come up with the perfect solution."

"Which conundrum is that, Momma?" I asked her.

"What to do about Donut Hearts," she said with a hint of dismay in her voice. "What other difficult decision are you facing at the moment?"

"Grace and I are trying to figure out who killed Gary Shook," I reminded her.

"I have every confidence in the world that you'll be able to do that," she said.

"Well, that makes one of us."

"Hey, I think you can do it, too," Phillip protested from the kitchen.

"Then it's settled: I'm going to be able to solve the case, and soon, based on the confidence you two have in me," I told them with a smile. I'd been trying to distract Momma from her original topic she'd wanted to discuss, for all the good it would do me. It might not have been the most flattering analogy, but when she had something on her mind, she was like a dog with a bone. I couldn't really complain though, since I'd gotten my tenacity from her.

"I'm talking about Donut Hearts," she said.

"Dot, I didn't think you were going to go through with that," Phillip chided her gently.

"As much as I appreciate your advice, dear, I've decided to go forward regardless."

He shrugged. "Suit yourself. If you two need me, I'll be out on the front porch, counting fireflies."

"While you're at it, do the lightning bugs, too," I told him with a grin. That was what I'd always called the little intermittent night-lights of summer I still loved.

"I have a hunch it will be the same number," he said with a grin.

"Before you go, Phillip, what do *you* think I should do?" I asked my stepfather.

"I'm sure you're getting better advice than I can give you," he said, brushing my request off as just a polite question and not a serious inquiry.

"Your opinion matters to me, too," I told him firmly. "I honestly want to know."

Phillip nodded, glanced at Momma for a moment, and then he said, "If I were you, I wouldn't do it. Not any of it. You're too young to quit. Every life needs a purpose, and that donut shop is yours, at least for the foreseeable future. Don't keep it on my account, though. It has to be your call."

"Thanks for sharing your opinion with me," I told him sincerely.

"You're welcome." He hesitated at the front door before he turned and added, "Thanks for asking."

"It really does mean the world to him that you asked him," Momma told me after he was gone. "He's quite fond of you, Suzanne."

"To tell the truth, I'm kind of fond of him myself, though sometimes I still can't believe it. You don't agree with him though, do you?"

Her lips formed two thin lines. "I never said that."

"No, but it was implied by his comment," I said. I braced myself and then told her, "Go ahead, Momma. Say what you have to say."

"I believe you should sell the shop to Emma and Sharon," she said firmly. "You're *never* going to get a better offer, so it makes sense financially, and I always believed that you were capable of much greater things than running Donut Hearts, as admirably as you've managed it so far."

"Was that an actual compliment about my business savvy?" I asked her with a grin.

"It was," she said. "In fact, it brings up a matter I've been considering for some time. Suzanne, how would you like to be part of *my* business ventures?"

"Hang on. Are you seriously asking me to be your partner?" My mother had more money and connections in our part of the state than I could even guess at. I knew she was constantly working in real estate, as well as other ventures, but I had no idea what all that entailed, and I had a feeling not even her husband knew all of the pies she owned pieces of in our part of the world.

"A junior partner, but a partner nonetheless," Momma said. "I'm getting older, and there are things I'm not able to do that I once could. I need someone I trust to work with me, and there's no one in the world I trust as much as you. You'd be amazed how good it feels to make things happen."

"I honestly don't know what to say," I answered honestly. "I feel honored, but we both know that I'd be in over my head."

"I won't throw you into the deep end and make you sink or swim," she said. "I'd start you off with a few acquisitions and take over some of my charitable work as well."

"You do charitable work?" I asked her, surprised by the news.

"My darling daughter, I've managed to acquire a great deal of wealth over the years," she admitted. "More than enough to pass on to you and Phillip when my time is up, so I like to make donations where I think they can do the most good. I only have one caveat to anyone who receives money from me: they aren't allowed to tell anyone else where it originated. I honestly believe that if giving isn't anonymous, it is worthless, at least to the giver."

"So that's why I've never seen your name on a building," I said.

"Or any other structures or facilities in the area," she agreed. "You would be under the same caveat. Could you do that?"

"How do you know that I don't already?" I asked her. While it was true that Jake and I gave more than our share to causes and charities we believed in, we had the same condition we applied to our own donations. If anyone, and I mean anyone, mentioned that we'd donated to them, they would be off our list forever. There were no second chances in that respect.

Momma looked equally surprised and pleased. "Of course. Well, what do you say? Together we could do great things, Suzanne."

I hugged her fiercely before stepping back. "Momma, that's probably the nicest thing you've ever said to me."

"I mean every word of it. This is a serious offer. So, what do you say? Are you ready to leave Donut Hearts behind and work on some truly great projects with me?" When I didn't answer right away, she smiled and added, "Child, are you actually *speechless*?"

"I believe I am," I told her. "In my defense, it's a lot to take in."

"You don't have to give me an answer at the moment," she said. "I just wanted you to know that there were other options for you out in the world besides running Donut Hearts."

"It hasn't been *all* bad," I reminded her.

"Suzanne, without the experience you've garnered running it, I *never* would be making you this offer. You've cut your teeth on that business and learned a great deal in the process. Now it's time to use those skills for bigger and better things."

"Thank you, Momma," I said. The table was clear, and I offered, "Is there anything else I can do for you at the moment? I really will give it careful thought."

"I know you will. For now, just go home, sleep on it, and we'll talk tomorrow," she said.

"I can do that," I said.

Chapter 19

I HAD TO CALL JAKE, and it couldn't even wait until I got back to the cottage. I hoped that tonight of all nights, he was free to speak with me.

He picked up on the second ring. "Hey, Suzanne. How goes the investigation?"

"Slow but sure," I told him, just happy to hear his voice. "Do you have a few minutes? I need to talk to you about something else."

"Absolutely. Give me a minute, and I'll call you right back."

"Okay," I said. I drove the short way home, and I was just walking up the front porch steps when my cell phone rang.

"Sorry about that. I had to handle one little thing. You've got my full attention now. What's up?"

"I'm not taking you away from anything important, am I?" I asked him, feeling a bit guilty about unloading my problems on him when he already had more than enough on his plate as it was.

"There's not a thing in the world I need to be doing at this moment. I'm ready when you are."

"I've had three offers today that involve our future, and I don't know what to do," I said, letting the words cascade out of my mouth in a rush.

"Wow, that's a busy day. What kind of offers are we talking about?"

"Emma and Sharon want to buy Donut Hearts outright, Jennifer from my book club wants to buy it and keep me on as the manager, and Momma wants me to sell it to Emma and Sharon and come to work for her. Jake, what am I going to do?"

"Hang on a second. Let me at least catch my breath," Jake answered.

"It's crazy, isn't it?" I asked him.

"It's not *that* crazy," he said. "I've been expecting your mother to try to recruit you for years."

"Seriously? That thought never even crossed my mind."

"Suzanne, you are running a small business successfully against great odds, you have a good business sense, and you are someone your mother trusts implicitly. Why *wouldn't* she want you on her team?"

"I don't know. I just never dreamed that I was on her level," I said.

"You probably aren't, at least not yet," Jake said honestly. "I'm guessing that she didn't offer you an equal partnership, did she?"

There was a reason my husband was such a successful detective. "I'd be junior to her, at least in the beginning, but it would still be a great deal of responsibility."

"I'm sure it would be, but I'm equally certain that it wouldn't be anything that you couldn't handle."

"Jake, is that what you think I should do?" I asked him. I was a grown woman, more than capable of making my own decisions, but my husband's opinion mattered more to me than anyone else's in the world, and that was saying something.

"Whoa. Cool your jets, girl. I think nothing of the sort. We're just talking here."

"Then what do you think I should do? Take Emma's offer or go with Jennifer?"

"Do you really want to know what I think?"

"Of course I do," I said.

"Then I'd choose between Emma and your mother. You don't want Jennifer's offer. Selling the donut shop and giving up control of it but having to work there all the while is a nonstarter as far as I'm concerned. You're welcome to go that route, but I'd advise against it."

"That's fair enough. Momma said the same thing," I said. "I'd *hate* working for anyone else at a place I built into what it is today."

"Then that's off the table," he said with a laugh. "See? We're already a third of the way home. It's an option to sell out and turn your mother down too, you know. Again, not giving advice, just pointing out possibilities. The last one is to do nothing and to continue on as you have been, and I think that has its own pluses and minuses."

"The money would be nice though," I said. "We could travel, get some expensive toys, and have enough not to worry about money for a very long time."

"That should be the *last* thing on your mind," Jake said. "We don't *need* a lot of money to be happy. We've proven that. I want you to feel fulfilled, if that's possible. As long as we're together, I'll have beans and cornbread every night and smile with every bite."

"I feel the same way," I said.

"I'm happy to hear that. How *is* the investigation going, by the way? Give me some details."

"We've eliminated two of our six main suspects. They have a troubling story, but as far as the murder goes, we've cleared them."

"Everyone seems to have drama in their lives these days," he said. "Except for me. My life's a picnic in the park."

"How's your family doing?" I asked him, hesitant to even ask.

"Don't get me started. Sarah's gotten herself tangled up with a guy who's at least trying to do his best, but Paul's rebelling again, and now Amy is flunking her summer school classes, not because she's not smart but because she's just not trying. It's a train wreck, and I can't fix any of it. That's the most frustrating part."

I didn't want to make the sacrifice, but I had to at least make the offer. "Jake, if I sell the donut shop and turn Momma down, we could spend more time in Raleigh with your family."

"That's a pretty noble offer, Suzanne, and I love you even more for making it, but I don't think my presence here would make much of a difference."

"I find that hard to believe," I said.

"Sadly, I'm afraid that it's true, though. It's starting to get through my thick head that they're going to have to figure things out for themselves without me. I'm not going anywhere, and if they need me, I'll come running, but they're going to have to make their own way. I don't like it, but there's really nothing I can do about it. Make this decision for yourself, Suzanne. You have my permission—shoot, my order—to be selfish. Don't consider *anyone* else's feelings, not mine, not your mother's, and not Emma's. How can she afford to buy you out, anyway?"

"She got an inheritance that she has to spend," I told him.

"Okay," he said, "good for her."

"So your advice is to be selfish," I summarized.

"That's it. But call Jennifer and tell her that deal isn't going to happen. It would make you miserable, and that would make me unhappy, so I blackball that one."

I laughed. "Who said you got a blackball?"

"I did," he replied happily. "I love you. You know that, right?"

"I do, and I feel the same way about you." As I started to hang up, I added, "Jake, don't be so hard on your family. They love you, too."

"Maybe so, but they've got a funny way of showing it lately. Let me know what you decide."

"You'll be at the top of my list," I told him, "day or night."

"Good. That's all I'm asking."

I felt better after talking to my husband, which was really no surprise. Jake had that effect on me. It would have been better having him there with me, but it was good enough.

I looked up a number on my phone and dialed. "Hey, Jennifer, it's not too late to be calling, is it?"

"Hardly," she laughed. "Then again, I'm not on Eastern Donut Time. You aren't taking me up on my offer, are you?"

"As much as I appreciate it, I'm going to have to decline," I said. "Are we okay?"

"We're better than okay," she said. "My husband backed my offer, but he told me that you'd be crazy to take it. Apparently he understands you better than I do."

"About this maybe, but not about books," I told her with a laugh. I was glad that I hadn't damaged the relationship we were just now trying to rebuild.

"Never about books. I can't wait to see you again and chat about what we've been reading."

"It's always been one of the highlights of my month," I told her.

"Good night, Suzanne."

"Good night, Jennifer, and thanks for reaching out to me again."

"I'm just sorry it took us all so long to do it. We agreed that *all* of our lives are better with you in them, and we can't say that about many people."

"I feel the same way about all three of you," I said as I ended the call. At least that part of my dilemma had been solved. That left the hardest choices still to make, but progress was progress.

Maybe tomorrow, I'd even have time to figure out who had killed Gary Shook. It was a great deal to hope for, but then again, stranger things had happened.

Today was proof of that if anything was.

The next morning, I woke up at my usual time, even though I wasn't scheduled to go to Donut Hearts, since it was one of the days Emma and Sharon ran the place. Unfortunately, sleep hadn't brought me any clarity as to what I should do, so I did the only thing I could think of.

I rolled over and went back to bed.

I awoke the second time a little after seven, which was definitely sleeping in for me, but hey, I had a lot of pressure on me at the moment, and it had definitely played a part in wearing me out. I grabbed a quick shower, started to make myself some breakfast, and then suddenly I didn't feel like being by myself anymore.

"Are you up?" I asked as Grace answered on the third ring.

"Yeah, I had to get up to answer the phone," she replied. "I'm just kidding. I've been up for twenty minutes. How about you? I'm guessing you've been up for three or four hours."

"As a matter of fact, I slept in this morning," I told her. "Do you feel like grabbing some breakfast at the Boxcar Grill this morning before we get started?"

"Do I ever," Grace said. "Should I drive over and pick you up?"

I was only a few hundred yards from Grace's place. "Why don't you walk up the road, and then we'll walk through the park together?" I suggested. "That way we can work up more of an appetite before we eat."

"Not much of one, but I'm game if you are. See you in a few."

I loved that my best friend was always up for just about anything. I grabbed my wallet and keys and then headed out to the porch to wait on her.

There was something on my glider, though. It was a piece of paper folded into thirds. What in the world was that about? I opened it with my hands shaking a bit, wondering if this was going to be a clue or a threat. I'd gotten both over the years I'd been digging into murder, and I couldn't imagine which one this might be.

It turned out to be a threat.

Definitely a threat.

Stop Digging or Start Dying.

"What's that?" Grace asked a few seconds later as I stared at the note, hoping it would tell me something new.

"I just got a message from someone who likes *The Shawshank Redemption*," I said.

She read it without touching it, a habit we'd both gotten into so we wouldn't leave too many extraneous fingerprints on clues and threats we'd received over the years. "I don't think so. The actual quote from the movie is 'Get busy living, or get busy dying.' It's completely different."

"Okay, maybe I'm mistaken about that part, but we're clearly getting too close for someone's taste," I said. "How do you know so much about that movie? I wouldn't think it would be your kind of flick."

"You know the kind of stuff I like," Grace said. "Stephen loves it though, and he's made me watch it with him four times. The things we do for love."

"I know what you mean," I said as I carefully refolded the note. "Hang on a second, I want to get a freezer bag for this."

"I'll come with you," she said as she followed me back inside the cottage. As I started to slide it into a large baggie, she asked, "Do you mind if I get a photo of it first?"

"That's a good idea," I said. I opened it back up, took a photo with my own phone, and after Grace was finished, I sealed it up. After that, I reached to the top shelf where I kept my cookbooks and tucked it between a copy of Fanny Farmer and Betty Crocker. They were two very important women in my cooking and baking life, and I never went long without consulting one or the other.

"Aren't we taking that with us to show Stephen?" she asked me.

"I doubt there will be any prints on it, but we can give it to him later to check," I said. "In the meantime, I don't feel like carrying what might be a clue around town and risk losing it."

"That's a fair point," she said. "Come on, I've got something to tell you."

"I hope it's good news," I said. "It feels like forever since I've had any of that kind."

"You get two offers for your shop in one day, and you don't call that good news?" she asked me.

"Three, actually. Momma wants me to sell the place and come to work for her."

"Wow, I was wondering when that would happen. Suzanne, will you still talk to me when you're rich?"

"I'm not going to be rich, and I haven't decided what I'm going to do yet," I admitted.

"If you don't want the job, can I have it?" she asked me.

"You'll have to take that up with Momma, but you know what a taskmaster she can be. Can you imagine being on her payroll?"

"Sure, for you maybe, but she likes *me*," Grace said with a grin.

"Who doesn't?" I asked, smiling in return.

"On second thought, I don't think I want to leave my job any time soon. I'm just starting to train my boss as it is."

"I don't blame you for that," I told her. "Come on. Let's get something to eat. You can tell me your news on the way."

We were in the park, which basically meant that we'd just left my front porch, when Grace told me, "Jenny didn't do it."

"What? How can you possibly know that?"

"There was a security camera in the shop across from her, and Stephen reviewed the tape. Jenny never left her post during the entire time in question. Oh, also, it's been narrowed down to a twenty-minute time frame now."

"Was Gary on the tape, too?"

"As a matter of fact, he was," she said. "He was seen speaking in camera range with Molly about something."

"Were they arguing by any chance?" I asked her hopefully.

"No, Stephen said it was something pretty blasé. She handed him a piece of paper, he double-checked it, and then he put it in his pocket. When Stephen asked her about it later, she told him it was her rent check, which the bank confirmed was cashed not half an hour before we found him."

"I can't believe he told you all that," I said.

"Hey, he's been a lot more cooperative lately. It took some time, but I think he'd rather have us on his side and not against him."

"Did you tell him anything new that we found?" I asked her.

"I told him everything," she said, clearly confused by my question. "Didn't we agree to do that ages ago?"

"Of course we did," I told her. "I just wish we had more to tell him."

"Are you kidding? He reconfirmed Lawrence and Cheryl's story too, including everything about her new ex-husband. In fact, he talked to a friend of his who's going to misplace some paperwork to buy them a few more hours before he gets out. I thought it was sweet of him."

"It is," I said. "I wonder if that's going to be enough to do them any good."

"Hey, we can only do what we can do. The rest is out of our hands," Grace answered with a shrug.

"Too true," I said as we got close to the Boxcar's front steps. "Come on. It's my treat," I said as I glanced over at Donut Hearts. They had a good crowd there, and I wondered if I'd ever be behind the counter again myself.

At least it was my decision and not someone else's, not that that mattered that much at the moment.

Chapter 20

"DID YOU HEAR THE GOOD news?" Jenny asked as we ran into her as we were going into the Boxcar Grill.

"We did. You're in the clear," I said. "Congratulations."

"That's not what I'm talking about, but thank you. Margaret, I mean Mom, has an alibi for the shortened time frame, so she's not a suspect anymore either."

It was clear that Jenny was happier about her birth mother's status than her own. I knew that I'd feel the same way if it had been my mother and me instead of them, but Margaret hadn't raised Jenny like Momma had raised me. Still, there was an undeniable bond between the two women.

"That is excellent news," Grace said. "When did this happen?"

"She just called and told me," she said excitedly. "We're going to Charlotte and going shopping since we don't have a shop to run anymore. Who knows? Maybe there's something to be said for starting over."

"Maybe there is," I said. Jenny hadn't been the only one at a turning point recently. Cheryl and Lawrence had decided to throw their old lives away and start off on a new adventure together, too. Was that what I needed to do? Had I grown stale in my job and my life, if I could forgive myself the pun?

Maybe it was time for me to make a major change myself.

"Are you coming?" Grace asked me as I was lost in thought. "If you'd like, I could always eat and meet you back out here."

"Hold your horses. I'm right behind you," I said with a smile.

"That a girl," she said as we both greeted Trish.

"Wow, this is a real honor having you two come by for breakfast," she said. "Lucky for you I've got a table right up front, so we can chat between customers."

"That *is* lucky," I said. It would mean we couldn't discuss the latest developments in the case, but having the opportunity to catch up with our friend was more than worth it.

Grace and I both ordered pancakes. I got two pieces of bacon while Grace got the sausage patties. "I'll swap one of my patties for a piece of your bacon," she suggested.

"Deal," I answered as Trish smiled.

"Should I have Hilda plate them up that way, or do you want to pick and choose which ones you trade?" she asked us happily. When she saw our grins, she answered her own question. "Yeah, I'm not about to get into the middle of that. You two can decide for yourselves."

She had to go refill some coffee cups after she placed our orders, so I took the opportunity to ask Grace, "What do you make of what Jenny said?"

"I think we're down to two real suspects now," she answered softly.

"Molly and Cynthia," I agreed. "Do you have a favorite?"

"Well, on the one hand, Molly had a lot more contact with Gary, so she might have had more reason to want to see him dead."

"But on the other," I finished for her, "Cynthia was clearly seen being threatened by the man in her own office."

"So right now, it's fifty-fifty," Grace said.

"How do we break the tie then?"

"I don't see that we have any choice. We go after *both* of them," Grace said. "And the more pressure we can put on them, the better."

"Agreed." I glanced at my watch. "I wonder if Momma's had a chance to check in with her sources yet."

"I doubt it. Not everybody is as early a bird as I am," she said with a grin. "Okay, as you are anyway. Tell you what. Let's eat breakfast and then give her a call."

"I don't know what I'm going to tell her about her offer," I hedged.

"Just tell her you need a little more time," Grace suggested. "She'll understand."

"You *know* she hates doing business with people who are indecisive," I reminded her.

"Sure, but you're her daughter, for land's sake."

"Maybe so, but business is business," I said.

"Then I'll call her for you. There, that's settled."

"No, I'll do it," I told her. "Thanks for the offer, but I can't keep ducking her until I make up my mind. It's not fair to me, and it's not fair to her either."

"That's even better," Grace answered with a smile as Trish came out of the kitchen carrying our food. How had she even gotten past us? I'd been so focused on what Grace had been telling me that I hadn't even noticed her. "Here comes breakfast."

"Whee," I said, drumming up as much enthusiasm as I could. It felt a little like a prisoner's last meal, because after it was over, I knew that I'd have to talk to Momma, and that was something I wasn't in any hurry to do.

"Hey, this isn't what I ordered," I said as I looked at my plate. There were indeed two pieces of bacon on it, and a sausage patty as well. I noticed that Grace's plate had an extra piece of bacon on it.

"Are you kidding me? It's the only way I'm going to be able to keep the peace at this table," Trish said with a laugh. "Enjoy. Those bonus sides are on the house."

"You're the best," I told her as I picked up one of my pieces of bacon and took a bite.

"That's what everybody says, and I haven't denied it even once," Trish answered.

After we finished the delicious pancakes and extras, we paid our bills and headed back out into the sunlight.

I'd put it off long enough.

It was time to call Momma to see if she'd been able to dig anything else up that might help us.

"Hey, Momma, is it too early for me to be calling?"

"Not at all," she said, and then she waited for me to continue. If she was hoping for news of my decision, she was going to be disappointed, but I wasn't about to bring it up if she didn't.

"Have you had a chance to call your sources yet?" I asked.

There was just a hint of hesitation in her voice as she quickly hid her first reaction. "I've reached out to them both, but neither one has gotten back to me yet...hold on. One is trying to call me right now. I'll be in touch soon," she said and then abruptly cut me off.

"She got a call while we were talking," I told Grace. "Let's go get my Jeep so we'll be ready to go when she calls us back."

I figured I'd hear from her by the time we got back to my cottage, but we still hadn't heard a word from her. As we sat in my Jeep, I said, "Any second now."

Grace looked at my phone and played a game we'd enjoyed as kids. "She's going to call back in three, two, one," and then she pointed at my phone.

It failed to ring on her command.

I waited a few seconds, and then I said, "You got the timing all wrong. Everybody knows that it's going to ring in three, two, one," and less than a moment later, my phone rang. "And that's how it's done," I said with a grin as I answered.

"Wow, that was quite a long call," I told her.

"He had to look into some records for me," Momma said, "but I've got a preliminary answer for you. Before I give it to you though, you need to promise me that you'll bring the police chief in on this with you. Suzanne, someone killed Gary Shook in the heat of the moment, and I don't want you two to be his next victims."

I didn't correct her pronoun use even though Grace and I were fairly certain that a woman had done the deed. We just didn't know which one had done it yet. "I promise," I said.

"Very well. From what I've been able to learn, the property was defaulted back to the bank four hours after the murder," Momma said.

"What? How is that even possible for them to work that quickly?"

"It was all perfectly legal, if a bit odd, but that's not the most unusual part of this," she explained.

"What could be odder than that?"

"There's already been a new buyer registered for the property," she said.

Now we were getting somewhere. For someone to have moved that quickly, they had to have inside information that the strip mall was going to revert to the bank due to a delinquent payment. "Who's buying it?" I asked her.

"Cynthia Logan is handling the expedited sale, probably in an effort to save her job. She's registered the preliminary buyer of record as Molly Davis."

"Thanks, Momma. We'll be in touch."

"I expect to hear from you soon, Suzanne, about more than just your investigation."

The meaning behind her statement was clear, but at that moment, I had other things on my mind. Grace and I were going to call Chief Grant and tell him what we'd just learned, but we were going to speak with the woman herself first.

"Molly is the one buying the strip mall," I told Grace as I headed toward the property in question. "She *had* to have been the one who killed Gary. The more I think about it, the more I believe that this wasn't a spur-of-the-moment act at all."

"Why do you say that?" she asked me.

"It wouldn't have been that easy for her to put the purchase together so quickly without knowing that it was going to be for sale soon," I said. "Molly runs a sewing shop. It would take a banker to know how to make things happen this quickly."

"Do you think Cynthia is in cahoots with her?" Grace asked.

"I suppose it's possible, but I believe that it's *more* likely that she's just a pawn in all of this." I really wanted a chance to speak with Molly before I called our chief of police, but the longer I drove, the more I realized that I couldn't break my promise to my mother. "Call Stephen and tell him where we're going and what we just found out."

"Seriously? We aren't going to speak with her first ourselves?" Grace asked, clearly confused by my request.

"I promised Momma," I said.

"Enough said," Grace answered as she pulled out her cell phone. After a brief conversation that covered the facts as we knew them, she hung up and said, "He's going to meet us there."

"I know it's not ideal, but I gave her my word," I said.

"No explanations or apologies are required," Grace said. "That's a sacred oath you gave her, and you can't break it."

"Thanks for understanding," I said.

We were half a mile from the strip mall when my phone rang again.

"Wow, when did you suddenly become so popular?" Grace asked me.

"Probably about the same time folks started wanting to buy Donut Hearts," I answered.

It was Momma again though, and I was thoroughly glad that I'd had Grace call Chief Grant first. "We're on our way to meet the chief at the strip mall," I said before she could say a word.

"I'm not quite sure that's where you need to go now," my mother told me.

"Why is that?"

"I heard from my second source, and there's a chance that Molly Davis isn't involved after all."

"But the sale of the property is going to be registered to her," I protested. "That makes her look guilty in my book."

"There's an issue with that, though. Molly hasn't signed the offer sheet yet."

"What does that mean?"

"Until it's registered at the bank and processed, Cynthia could substitute *anyone's* name she wants to as the buyer of record, since she's the one handling all of the paperwork," Momma explained.

And then it hit me. I suddenly realized that we'd been played all along, and we were still being led around by our noses. Cynthia Logan had been one step ahead of us the entire time, and I'd been too dense to see it.

"Thanks, Momma. I'll be in touch," I said as I made an abrupt U-turn and headed back to the cottage.

"Where are we going now?" Grace asked me.

"It doesn't appear that Molly had anything to do with it," I said. "Cynthia Logan has been treating us like fools from the start."

"Talk to me, Suzanne, but first, where are we going?"

"Back to the cottage. I want to get that note from this morning and confront her with it. As far as I know, it's the first mistake she's made, and I'm going to be sure she pays for it. Any objections?"

"You know me. I'm just going along for the ride," Grace answered. "Tell me why you think she's guilty though, if you don't mind."

"At the bank when Momma saw her arguing with Gary Shook, my hunch is that he refused to be bullied into selling her the property outright. Then things changed. I'm not sure what kind of leverage she had on him, but clearly she thought it was good enough when she confronted him in the storeroom of For The Birds. Maybe she threatened to foreclose on it after the missed payments, or maybe she promised to go to the police to have him arrested for something he'd tried with her. It wouldn't be that far of a leap to believe that Gary had attempted to pressure her, but without realizing it, he'd been trying to pet a tiger and not a kitten. For whatever reason, he refused her, and Cynthia knew that she'd have to do something even more aggressive. Maybe she went to see him on her lunch hour to try to threaten him again or to escalate the pressure in some other way. She could have easily followed him into that storeroom, and when he refused her again, she killed him, not in a fit of anger but in premeditation. I believe she went there with the intention of killing him all along."

"But why force the issue?"

"Maybe the real buyer was getting cold feet. I'm guessing Cynthia lied to him as well, representing that she controlled that property all along, not Gary. She could have seen it all falling apart before her very eyes, so she had to act, and she had to do it quickly. I'm not positive that's the truth, but it makes sense. When we see her, we'll have to ask her."

"What good is the note going to do us?" Grace asked.

"We're going to lie and say we found one of her fingerprints on it," I said. "If she folds, we can use it to bully her into telling us the truth," I said. "After all, it's just like Lawrence told us before. The only way to beat a bully is to bully them right back and show them that you won't back down."

"Should I call Stephen back?" she asked as I parked in front of the cottage and jumped out.

"Let's get that note first," I told her as I hurried up onto the porch.

"Go on. I'll stay here and be ready to call him when you get back," Grace said.

"I'll just be a second," I said as I unlocked the front door and rushed inside. I was worried that though I'd hidden the threatening note, Cynthia may have broken in and retrieved it, but it was exactly where I'd left it, right between Betty and Fanny. On my way out, I picked up a bottle of water. That sausage and bacon had made me thirsty.

I raced out the front door so we could head to the bank and confront Cynthia with the note tucked under my arm and then see what she had to say about what we'd learned so recently.

And then I saw her standing there right out in the open with Grace just in front of her.

My best friend's face was pale and her body was rigid, and at that moment, I noticed the gun pointing into her side.

It appeared that we were a day late and a dollar short with our detection, and this just might be the last time we faced off with a cold-blooded killer.

Chapter 21

"LET HER GO, CYNTHIA," I said as I started toward them.

I watched helplessly as the killer increased the pressure on Grace's ribs, making her flinch involuntarily.

"That's close enough," Cynthia said calmly. "Don't make me do something you're going to regret, Suzanne. Just give me that note, and I'll be on my way."

I knew there was zero chance she was going to let us go free, even if we did as we were told. That note was the *only* leverage we had, fingerprint or not. Why hadn't I told Grace to call the police chief *before* I went after it? I couldn't do anything about that now, but if something happened to my friend because of my stubbornness, I'd never be able to forgive myself. "It's still in the cottage," I said. "Let me go get it for you." If I could get back inside, I could call the police and maybe even get a weapon of my own. Jake kept a spare revolver under the stairs, and he'd made sure that I knew how to use it after all of the close calls I'd had in the past.

"Nice try," she said. "It's right there."

"I'm sorry," Grace said meekly. "I told her that's why we were here."

With a gun pointing at her, how could she do otherwise? "No worries. It's going to be okay, Grace." I just wished I had the confidence to actually believe what I was saying. We were in a jam, maybe the worst one we'd ever been in.

"Listen to Grace," Cynthia said calmly. "Give me the note, Suzanne."

"Why did you even leave it?" I asked her. "We weren't positive it was you at that point. You took a chance, didn't you?"

"I got the jitters," she said. "You kept showing up everywhere I was. When you walked into the bank yesterday, I thought for sure that you knew."

"And yet you still managed to keep your cool," I said. "You even made it look as though you were being chewed out by your boss. That wasn't what was happening at all, was it?"

"I was getting him to sign off on the quick sale," she answered happily. "He was so relieved that he didn't even want details on how I'd managed it. That fool Gary Shook didn't know what a gold mine he was sitting on. I could have resold that property myself to an investment group from Charlotte and made a fortune on it, but he wouldn't sell it to me, even though he was in arrears on his payments, so he had to go."

"It was a risk putting it in Molly's name on the paperwork though, wasn't it?" I asked as I weighed the chances of getting us both out of this mess alive. I still had a water bottle in my hand, and at least it was full, so if I used it correctly, I might be able to make a weapon out of it.

Then again, it would be taking an awful chance.

But what choice did I really have?

"I set up a dummy corporation to buy it weeks ago, and that name would have been the final owner listed on the paperwork," she said, "but in the meantime, I thought I might be able to use Molly to deflect suspicion away from me by putting her name on one of the preliminary documents. I'm guessing that it worked too, since there aren't any cops here right now."

"Why break into Gary's place?" I asked, trying to buy us some time so I could come up with a plan.

"He had something on me. What it was doesn't matter. It's gone now. You two are the last loose threads there are."

I didn't like the sound of that. "They'll know you did it soon enough when they start digging into your paper trail," I said. "Give yourself up, and we'll do our best to see that they go easy on you."

"It's a nice try, but that's not happening. Hand over the note, Suzanne. I'm getting tired of this little game." She jabbed the gun into Grace's ribs again, and I heard my friend grunt from the pain.

I had to do something, and it had to be right now.

"Here you go," I said as I took another step forward.

"Stop right where you are," she said fiercely. "We'll come to you." Cynthia shoved Grace forward and took her eyes off of my friend for an instant as she reached for the offered note.

It was now or never.

I screamed with all of my might as I drew back the bottle to hurl it at her head.

In that instant, I heard the gun go off, and I watched in slow-motion horror as Grace fell to the ground.

Cynthia had shot her! I'd tried to save her, but instead I might have been the one who had cost her her life.

I went into an insane frenzy the instant I saw Grace lying there helplessly. I threw that water bottle at Cynthia's head with everything I had, doing my best to kill her with it.

It struck Cynthia directly in the forehead and even seemed to stun her for a moment, so I took that single opportunity I had while she was distracted to rush her and get that gun out of her hands before she could fire it again.

To my surprise, she recovered quicker than I thought she would, and before I could get to her, she managed to get a shot off in my direction after all.

Almost before I heard the sound of the shot, I felt the sharp bite in my left arm, as though I'd been suddenly skewered with a molten shaft or red-hot iron.

That was when I heard another gun bark just behind her, and Cynthia went down in a heap beside Grace.

Though I was in agony, I pushed it all aside as I knelt down beside my best friend, not even caring who had come to our rescue and saved me in the end.

"Grace! Grace!" I screamed at her.

"Take it easy," she said as she opened her eyes and looked at me. "I don't know how it happened, but she must have missed me completely."

"If that's true, then why are you bleeding?" I asked her as I looked down at the stain growing on the right side of her blouse.

"Well, would you look at that," she said in wonder, and then she passed out.

Chapter 22

CHIEF GRANT RAN UP to Grace and bent over her, his weapon still drawn. "Is she dead?" His voice was completely devoid of all hope, and I knew that he feared the worst.

"I don't think so," I said as I leaned over her and found a pulse with my good hand. "Call an ambulance."

"It's on its way. She managed to call me without Cynthia knowing it. I heard most of what happened."

"How about Cynthia?" I asked as I looked over at her lifeless form.

"She's dead," he said matter-of-factly, as though he hadn't even had to check. If it registered with him that he'd just shot and killed the murderer, I couldn't tell.

The only thing he cared about was Grace, and I couldn't blame him.

It was all I was worried about, too.

He glanced over at me and seemed to see me for the first time. "Are you okay, Suzanne?"

"I'm fine," I said as a wave of pain came over me. "Maybe not," I said as I staggered a bit.

"Come on, lean on me," he replied as the ambulance pulled into my drive.

"Forget about me. Take care of her," I answered as I motioned to Grace.

"We're going to take care of both of you," he said.

Chapter 23

"HOW'S SHE DOING?" I asked the chief as he came into my room later that night. The bullet that had hit me had gone straight through the fleshy part of my arm, a through-and-through, the doctor had called it, and while it still hurt a great deal, it had somehow made it through me without doing much damage.

"She's going to be fine. There's something she needs to tell you, but she'll only do it in person." Grace had been lucky as well, in her own way. It seemed that neither of Cynthia's shots had done nearly as much harm as she'd clearly intended. The bullet intended to kill Grace had just grazed her side.

Maybe the distraction I'd made had done some good after all.

"I want to see her," I said as I tried to get up.

It didn't work. If I got shot in the arm, why were my legs so weak?

"You're in luck then, because they're bringing her here in just a minute," he answered. "It looks like you're going to have yourself a roommate."

I felt a flood of relief go through me. "I'm so glad," I said. "Thank you, Stephen, for saving our lives, for everything."

"You're welcome," he said, clearly uncomfortable with the sentiment. "I was just doing my job."

"You did more than that, and we both know it," I said.

"Don't kid yourself. You did enough to distract her twice to let me get a clear shot. Otherwise it would have had a completely different outcome, and we both know it. You're the hero here, not me. I had a gun. All you had was a bottle of water."

"Well, you know what they say. It's important to hydrate." I tried to smile, but I was still in some pain even with the meds they'd given me.

He was about to say something when Momma and Phillip burst into the room. The chief stepped out to give us some privacy, which was kind of him. "Suzanne, are you all right? They wouldn't let us see you until now!"

"I'm battered and bloody, but I'm still standing, and apparently so is Grace," I told her.

Momma looked down at me and frowned. "This has been happening much too often lately for my taste, young lady."

"Mine, too," I said. "You'll be happy to know that as of this moment, I'm officially through with this amateur detective business. This one was too close for comfort even for me."

"You've said that before," she reminded me.

"Maybe so, but this time I mean it. Did somebody call Jake?"

"He's on his way," Phillip said. "I'll step out into the hallway and let you two have a little privacy. I'm glad you're okay, Suzanne."

"Thanks. Come here and give me a kiss on the cheek," I ordered him.

There were tears in his eyes as he leaned over and kissed my forehead instead. "I love you, kiddo. You know that, right?"

"I love you, too," I said, and then all three of us were crying.

At that moment, Emma and Sharon rushed in. "Are you okay?"

"I'm fine," I said, wiping away my tears with my good hand.

"We'll leave you all alone then," Emma said as she started to back out, sensing the mood of the room.

"Hang on a second. There's something I need to tell you all first."

"Suzanne, we don't have to talk about that right now," Emma said.

"Yes, we do," I said. "As much as I appreciate your offer, I can't sell Donut Hearts, not to you, and not to anyone else." Just saying it took a weight off of me. My donut shop was where I belonged, and while I might sell it someday, it wouldn't be anytime soon. All I wanted right now was to see Jake, get better, and then go back to Donut Hearts, in that order.

"We figured that," Emma said with a smile. "It was a long shot, and we knew it. Now it's on to Plan B."

"What's Plan B?" I asked, happy that she'd taken the news so well.

"Barton is going to open an upscale restaurant at a spot halfway between April Springs and Union Square," she said. "He just doesn't know it yet."

Sharon agreed. "We decided that if you said no, this would be perfect. It will keep everyone we love close." I was sure that was her main priority, so it would have worked out for her either way.

"Do you think he'll do it?" I asked.

"There's no doubt in my mind," Emma said. "Anyway, we just wanted to check on you. See you later, boss."

"I have one favor to ask you," I said before they could go.

"Just name it," Emma said.

"Would you two mind running Donut Hearts for me until I'm able to heal enough to take back over myself?" I asked them.

"We'd be honored," Emma said, and Sharon nodded in agreement.

Once they were gone, I turned to my mother. "Are you okay with my decision?"

"To quit detecting?" she asked me with a smile. "I'm all for it."

"I'm talking about staying at Donut Hearts for the time being," I chided her lightly.

"I couldn't be happier for you," she said. "Now let's leave this child alone and let her get some rest," Momma said as she took Phillip's hand.

I didn't know how long I was alone, because I actually managed to drift off for a bit. Those must have been some good meds.

I woke up as someone opened the door to my room.

I'd been hoping that it was Jake, but I was almost as happy to see that it was Grace instead, being wheeled in on a bed.

"Hey, roomie," I told her. "How are you feeling?"

"Like I got shot in the side," she said with a weak grin. "How about you?"

"About the same," I admitted. Her smile didn't go away. "You don't seem all that upset about it, to be honest with you."

"Oh, I hated that part of it, but at least something good came out of it," she said as Chief Grant walked in with Jake at his side.

My husband hugged me gently, and then he asked softly, "Are you okay?"

"I'm fine and dandy now," I said. "You should know that I turned everyone down. I'm going to keep owning and running Donut Hearts until further notice. Are you good with that?"

"I'm golden," he said. "That was actually what I was hoping you'd do."

Grace spoke up. "I hate to interrupt your reunion, but Stephen and I need a favor from you both."

"All you have to do is name it," I said. "You don't even have to ask."

"This one is easy. We want you to be our witnesses. We're getting married."

"That's wonderful news," I said with real joy in my heart. Those two belonged together just as surely as Jake and I did. "When's the big day?"

"In about ten minutes, or at least as soon as the preacher can get here," she said.

"Don't you need a license to do that legally?" Jake asked them. "Not that I'm not happy for you both."

"I've got it right here," Stephen said as he patted his pocket. "It's open-ended, so all I have to do is fill in the date."

"How long have you been carrying that around with you?" I asked him.

"About six months," he admitted. "I got tired of asking, so the last time I told Grace if we were ever going to get hitched, she was going to have to be the one who proposed."

Grace grinned at me from her slightly inclined bed. "I thought it would be a dramatic gesture as they wheeled me into the emergency room, but the joke was on me. I pulled through."

Stephen Grant laughed. "I'm holding her to it, though. I've got witnesses, so she can't back out now."

"We both know that's the last thing I want to do," Grace said as she looked at him with love.

It was one of the most beautiful ceremonies I'd ever seen in my life, even though it took place in a hospital room with both the bride and the maid of honor confined to their beds. The joy was strong and heart-felt, and love filled the room.

They weren't going to have much of a honeymoon, even though I'd jokingly offered to move to another room for the night. Grace told me that there would be time enough for that once we were all recovered, and I realized that there were going to be changes in all of our lives.

Second chances were too precious to waste, and I didn't plan on risking mine ever again.

At least that was my plan.

RECIPES

Cinnamon Applesauce Donuts

Since Hilda has been experimenting in this book with apples and Suzanne makes a special batch of cinnamon donuts for one of her customers, I thought I'd take the best of both worlds and offer this baked donut recipe to you. It's a real winner, and if you've never tried to make baked donuts in your oven before, this is a good place to start. You don't even need a muffin tin or a donut pan for this one, since the donuts bake on a standard cookie sheet. Give them a try, and if you're feeling particularly adventurous, try spreading a little cinnamon apple butter on top of these while they're still warm!

Ingredients

2 packets dry yeast

1/2 cup warm water

1/2 cup white granulated sugar

1 1/2 cups applesauce (use cinnamon-flavored applesauce for an extra boost of flavor!)

3 tablespoons salted butter, melted

2 teaspoons cinnamon

1 teaspoon nutmeg

1/4 teaspoon salt

2 eggs, lightly beaten

5 1/2 to 6 1/2 cups all-purpose flour

Topping

1/2 cup salted butter, melted

1/2 cup white granulated sugar

1 tablespoon cinnamon

or

1 cup cinnamon apple butter

Directions

In a large bowl, dissolve the yeast in the warm water, allowing it to sit 5 minutes. Add sugar, applesauce, melted butter, cinnamon, nutmeg, salt, beaten eggs, and 3 cups of the flour. Beat this mixture at low speed until it is mixed well, then beat on medium speed for another minute.

By hand, use a heavy wooden spoon to stir in enough of the remaining flour slowly until the mixture forms a soft dough, approximately 2 1/2 more cups.

Turn this out onto a lightly floured surface and knead for 5 minutes.

Place the dough back in the bowl after coating the surface with cooking spray, cover, and let sit in a warm place free from drafts for about an hour or until doubled in size.

Punch the dough down and then roll it out on a well-floured surface to about 1/2 inch thick, then cut out any shape you prefer, whether with a round cutter or a standard cookie cutter for fun.

Place the dough on a well-greased baking sheet and then brush the tops with melted butter. Cover and let rise again for 30 minutes.

In the meantime, preheat your oven to 425 degrees F and bake until golden brown, approximately 8 to 12 minutes depending on your oven.

After removing to a cooling rack, brush the tops with melted butter and then dip them in the topping of your choice.

Makes 10 to 14 donuts, depending on the size you make.

When a Donut Isn't Really a Donut
(But it's still really good!)

This is my go-to recipe when I don't feel like going to much trouble. Let's face it: we all feel that way sometimes, and I'm no exception. You can get creative with the basic recipe and include all kinds of things like dried fruits and nuts, or you can eat them plain with a bit of butter (okay, a lot of butter) slathered on top.

Ingredients

1 can refrigerated canned biscuit dough, your choice

1/4 cup dried fruit or nuts, or no additions at all

Oil for frying

Enough canola oil to fry the donuts in.

Directions

These couldn't be simpler.

Heat enough canola oil to fry the dough to 375 degrees F.

While you are waiting for the oil to come to temperature, open the can of dough and separate the biscuits into individual servings. If you'd like, pry them apart and add some filling into each one, or make them plain.

If you add fruit or nuts, be sure to seal the edges carefully after placing the filling in the center of the biscuit. It is best to use approximately 1 tablespoon of filling inside each biscuit.

Fry the biscuits in the hot oil, being careful not to crowd them, for about 4 minutes, flipping halfway through, or until both sides are golden brown.

Drain on paper towels and enjoy, dusting the tops with powdered sugar or simply using melted butter as a topping in and of itself.

Makes as many biscuits as are in the tube, which varies.

Momma's Pot Roast

Since Suzanne's mother serves her pot roast in the book, I thought I'd share my favorite pot roast recipe with you. It is one of my slow-cooker favorites! There are several variations you can try, but I like this version the best. When it's finished, the meat falls apart to the touch, and the veggies are tender delights. This is a great recipe year-round, so don't just make it when it's cold outside. Plus, the house smells delightful as this meal is cooking, and by the time it's ready, we're all eager to dive in!

Ingredients

1 boneless beef chuck roast (2 to 3 pounds, but any large cut of roast will do)

3 tablespoons all-purpose flour

2 teaspoons seasoning (I like Montreal Steak)

1/4 cup canola oil, or enough to cover the bottom of your skillet

1 can beef broth (14.5 oz.)

2 tablespoons salted butter

1 onion, coarsely chopped

1 can condensed cream of mushroom soup (10 3/4 oz.)

Baby bella mushrooms, sliced (10 oz.)

2 bay leaves

3 tablespoons all-purpose flour

1 package baby carrots (16 oz.)

6 to 10 new potatoes (they are small, and we like Yukon gold, but any small potato will do)

Directions

Rub the roast on all six sides with the flour mixed with the seasoning of your choice.

Over medium-high heat, sear the roast on all six sides until it's browned all over. Place the browned roast in the bottom of the slow cooker. Add the beef broth to the hot pan and deglaze it, stirring over low heat. Pour this mixture onto the meat in the slow cooker, but don't add any additional water!

In the skillet you just used, melt the butter and sauté half the coarsely chopped onion until it browns slightly. Spoon out the cream of mushroom soup on top of the roast.

Spoon the sautéed onions on top of the soup and then add the rest of the raw onion, coarsely chopped. Add half the mushrooms, sliced, to the slow cooker. Add two bay leaves. Cook for 3 hours on high.

After 3 hours, add the baby carrots, the new potatoes, and the remainder of the mushrooms (sliced) to the mix.

Continue cooking for 3 more hours on high, and then enjoy!

Cinnamon Nuggets

These treats are good year-round, but we especially like them when it's cool outside.

They are especially good with hot chocolate, but have them with your favorite beverage of choice and you can't go wrong!

Ingredients

1 egg, lightly beaten

1/2 cup whole milk (2% will do)

1/4 cup sugar, white granulated

1/8 cup oil (canola is my favorite)

Sifted

1 cup flour, unbleached all-purpose

2 teaspoons baking powder

2 teaspoons cinnamon

1 teaspoon nutmeg

1/4 teaspoon salt

Oil

Canola oil for frying (the amount depends on your pot or fryer)

Directions

In one bowl, beat the egg thoroughly, then add the milk, sugar, and canola oil to the mix.

In a separate bowl, sift together the flour, baking powder, cinnamon, nutmeg, and salt. Add the dry ingredients to the wet, mixing well until you have a smooth consistency. This will make a soft batter more than a dough, so don't be alarmed if it's a bit sticky.

Drop bits of dough using a small-sized cookie scoop (about the size of your thumb).

Fry in hot canola oil (360° to 370°F) for 1 1⁄2 to 2 minutes, turning halfway through.

Drain on paper towels and then dust with powdered sugar or even hot chocolate mix.

Yield: 12 to 16 donut holes

If you enjoy Jessica Beck Mysteries and you would like to be notified when the next book is being released, please visit our website at jessicabeckmysteries.net for valuable information about Jessica's books, and sign up for her new-releases-only mail blast.

Your email address will not be shared, sold, bartered, traded, broadcast, or disclosed in any way. There will be no spam from us, just a friendly reminder when the latest book is being released, and of course, you can drop out at any time.

Other Books by Jessica Beck

The Donut Mysteries
Glazed Murder
Fatally Frosted
Sinister Sprinkles
Evil Éclairs
Tragic Toppings
Killer Crullers
Drop Dead Chocolate
Powdered Peril
Illegally Iced
Deadly Donuts
Assault and Batter
Sweet Suspects
Deep Fried Homicide
Custard Crime
Lemon Larceny
Bad Bites
Old Fashioned Crooks
Dangerous Dough
Troubled Treats
Sugar Coated Sins
Criminal Crumbs
Vanilla Vices
Raspberry Revenge
Fugitive Filling
Devil's Food Defense
Pumpkin Pleas
Floured Felonies
Mixed Malice

Tasty Trials
Baked Books
Cranberry Crimes
Boston Cream Bribes
Cherry Filled Charges
Scary Sweets
Cocoa Crush
Pastry Penalties
Apple Stuffed Alibies
Perjury Proof
Caramel Canvas
Dark Drizzles
Counterfeit Confections
Measured Mayhem
Blended Bribes
Sifted Sentences
Dusted Discoveries
Nasty Knead
Rigged Rising
Donut Despair
Whisked Warnings
Baker's Burden
The Classic Diner Mysteries
A Chili Death
A Deadly Beef
A Killer Cake
A Baked Ham
A Bad Egg
A Real Pickle
A Burned Biscuit
The Ghost Cat Cozy Mysteries
Ghost Cat: Midnight Paws

Ghost Cat 2: Bid for Midnight
The Cast Iron Cooking Mysteries
Cast Iron Will
Cast Iron Conviction
Cast Iron Alibi
Cast Iron Motive
Cast Iron Suspicion
Nonfiction
The Donut Mysteries Cookbook